I write fun, flirty fiction with feisty heroines and a bit of an edge. Writing romance is cool because I get to wear pretty shoes instead of wellies. I live in a mountain kingdom in Derbyshire, where my family and pets are kind enough to ignore the domestic chaos. Happily, we're in walking distance of a supermarket. I love hearts, flowers, happy endings, all things vintage, most things French. When I'm not on Facebook and can't find an excuse for shopping, I'll be walking or gardening. On days when I want to be really scared, I ride a tandem.

You can follow me on Twitter @janelinfoot.

The Right Side
of Mr Wrong

JANE LINFOOT

Harper*Impulse* an imprint of
HarperCollins*Publishers Ltd*
77–85 Fulham Palace Road
Hammersmith, London W6 8JB

www.harpercollins.co.uk

A Paperback Original 2014

First published in Great Britain in ebook format by HarperImpulse 2013

A catalogue record for this book
is available from the British Library

ISBN: 9780007591718

This novel is entirely a work of fiction.

Au

For M and D ♥

Prologue

Brando Marshall catapulted out of the lift, and cursed that he was late for his midday summons to Bryony's flat. He rapped on her door, and braced himself for whatever was coming. Only one thing was certain – with baby sister Bryony, there was no such thing as a free lunch.

'Brando!' Tall, blonde, beautiful and air kissing, Bryony grinned, then grappled him into a hug that squished his breath away. Definitely a bad sign.

'So. Long time, no see.' She patted his arm as she released him.

What the hell? She was the one who'd been avoiding him.

'Not still cross about Country House Crisis are you Brando?'

No, not cross. Incandescent, more like.

They both knew she was the one person in the world he couldn't refuse, but letting the TV crew into Edgerton Manor to fill a gap in her schedule, was a huge favour she should have respected.

'There's a lot to answer for Bry. You said a few shots to show the downside of owning a stately home, and a few business ideas from the presenter.' Not that *he* needed business advice, but that was the point of the thing. 'I play along, then instead of gruesome Gloria coming out with her usual bed and breakfast in the stable block bollocks, she says what I need is a wife, and invites the world to apply for the job! Tell me, what part of that would

1

I not be fuming about?'

The whites of Bryony's eyes contained more desperation than her coaxing tone. 'Come through, have some lunch…'

He followed her into the lofty living space, with its spectacular view of the Thames, and she gestured towards the long granite breakfast bar.

One corporate sandwich platter which screamed television company expenses, one showy vase of flowers and he had her rumbled.

'You hate sandwiches at lunchtime Bry, and you'd never choose *orange* lilies. What's going on?'

He watched her face crumple. Damn the way that expression always made him feel responsible.

'Jeez, what's he doing here?' He grimaced as a guy with a camera on his shoulder emerged from behind the giant fridge.

'Please Brando…' her squeak became quietly urgent. 'We're making a Country House Crisis follow-up, and I need you to give me one more Lord of the Manor shot. That's all, it's not much to ask, but there's a huge amount at stake for me here.'

No emotional blackmail at all then. He counted to ten under his breath.

Then caved. 'Okay, dammit! I *knew* I could smell a waxed jacket!'

Plucking a coat from behind a sofa, she tossed it towards him. 'Put the Barbour on and come to the table. We're ready to go, as soon as you are.'

Nice ambush Bryony.

Dragging on the coat, he sidled forwards, aware of the cameraman behind him now.

'The table's perfect for this shot, because we've had such a huge response… you remember Brando? A wife needed for Edgerton Manor, applications on a postcard.'

Gloria Rutherford trying to bounce him to the altar on national TV would be etched upon Brando's memory until the end of time. But he wasn't about to admit it.

Bryony arrived beside him, arms wrapped around a wide box. With one flip, she sent a cascade of postcards whooshing across the table. 'There were over five hundred entries, you really caught the public imagination – in terms of viewing figures, it's sensational.'

'What the...' Brando winced as the array of potential brides fanned out in front of him, and made his head swim. 'This is insane.'

Bryony cut in hastily. 'No Brando, it's successful TV, and you *have* to help. Just choose one!' The note in her voice slid upwards. 'And don't you dare run out on me!'

He'd heard that note before, when they were kids, practically those same words, making his chest twang the same way it did now. That one note of desperation spun him right back to when he was about to walk out and leave her, simply because he couldn't stand to stay at home any more. He had saved himself, and left her behind, and the guilt still burned fresh, which was why he could never say 'no' now, whatever she asked him. Although that didn't mean it didn't drive him round the bend every time it happened.

'Jeez, what sort of woman would want to do this anyway?' He swallowed hard to dispel the distaste.

'Go on then.' Chivvying beside him, Bryony's voice was lighter, now she sensed she was about to get what she wanted.

As she reached over to swirl the ocean of colour, he caught sight of a card. One image. Incongruous. Nothing to do with brides or weddings.

He leaned in, plucked it from the pile, held it in his palm. A blast from the past. For a fraction of a second his face cracked into a smile, then he tossed the card back on the table.

'Thanks Brando. I owe you.' She flashed him a grateful smile which melted into a slow grin. 'You know Gloria's right though?'

'Meaning?'

'You're thirty five, a wife would be great for you.'

'You have to be joking?'

One blink of Bryony's clear blue eyes said she was not only

serious, but back on his case. 'And a little bit more footage from Edgerton, would make all the difference too. You with your trial wife perhaps?'

Now he'd heard it all. Would she never back off?

'Okay, Bry, I'll say this one time only. This far I've done what you wanted, but as of now I'm through with this, out. That's O-U-T as in "I'm having zero involvement." Understand?'

'I'm only thinking of you – and your long-term happiness.' Bryony, as usual, giving it everything she'd got.

'For happiness, read TV rankings?' He gave a bitter laugh. Deep down he knew her concern was genuine, but she had to butt out. 'I'm a lost cause, you're wasting your time.'

'Brando...'

He gritted his teeth, hardened himself to her wail. 'Sorry Bry, but I'm done here.' He screwed out of the jacket, making a lunge for the door. 'And that means, no more Country House Crisis, no TV crews, but most of all, NO WIFE!'

Chapter One

Sorry, no matrimonial ambitions whatsoever, but great at organising...

For the ninety-ninth time that afternoon Shea Summers wondered how those few short words she'd scribbled on a postcard had catapulted *her* into the air. Private helicopters didn't happen every day, even in affluent North Cheshire, at least not to her.

Brando Marshall, of Edgerton Manor, in need of a wife, applications on a postcard. Women had been fighting for the opportunity apparently. It seemed ironic that she was the one the TV company had chosen, when she didn't give a damn about it, and had zero intention of becoming anyone's wife.

She clutched her stomach as it gave another unnerving lurch. Beneath her white knuckles it was performing the same impromptu tango it had before her first ever dancing exam when she was seven, the same one it did every time she psyched herself up now, as a wimpy twenty four year old, for the misery of a bikini wax. And she had an idea that a bikini wax might be a walk-in-the-park compared to what she had let herself in for here. She delved into the pocket of her tailored jacket in search of fortification, and gesticulated wildly, in the direction of the co-pilot.

'Fancy a sour worm, or a pink shrimp?'

The co-pilot, turned, ran an eye swiftly up her legs, then winked as he gave a half shake of his head. She returned his grin, slipped

5

a sour worm into her mouth, and shuddered as the sugar hit zapped her taste buds. Then she shuddered again as she took in the panorama below. Worryingly green. Green as in rural, rolling countryside. Green as in miles from anywhere.

Damn. She definitely hadn't expected a middle-of-nowhere scenario. Her insides squished as she recalled all the stuff she hadn't asked. Bryony, the nice girl from the TV company, had been very persuasive and reassuring, but she hadn't let her get a word in edgeways.

'Just a bit of that organising you're obviously so good at and a few pieces to camera... a new angle for the follow-up programme... Brando is very rarely there... you could make it your holiday...'

'Closing in now Miss Summers!'

The pilot's gruff tones hauled her back to the present with a jerk that caused her to gulp her last pink shrimp practically whole. A weird shiver of déjà-vu slithered down her back as she peered down at the collection of stone-tiled roofs flashing gold in the autumn sun, took in a classical facade of the elegant house with its perfect rhythm of Georgian sash windows. The same spinning view of Edgerton Manor she'd last seen on the closing credits of the Country House Crisis programme. As she took in the real-life extent of the property her heart faltered. She hoped she hadn't over-exaggerated her organisational skills. She was used to working in big houses, but this one was something else.

Dragging her eyes away from the view below, she brushed the sugar dust off the pleats of her skirt, slipped her feet back into the patent stilettos she'd eased out of earlier, and dug the spike of the heel softly into her ankle. Just enough pain to remind her she wasn't dreaming, without the nightmare of a ripped stocking. She wasn't sure that helicopters mixed with towering court shoes, but she knew if she could only nail that all-important first impression, the rest was usually easy-peasy.

'Almost there now, I'll be bringing us down on the grassy area in front of the house, Miss Summers.'

She hurled a mental pillow over the voice in her head which was yelling 'Eeeeeeeek', snatched up her bag and made a grab for her lip gloss and her heavily framed Dolce & Gabbana glasses.

'Oh, lordy, look at that!' She stifled a groan of dismay. Grassy had to be a man's way of describing the expanse of mud where they were about to land.

Mud and high heels. Not the best combination.

Wriggling her skirt into place, she tugged her jacket into submission over her cleavage, and widened her smile to the max. So much for her impressive entrance, it was going to take a miracle just to get her to the front door.

* * *

'Dropping women onto me out of the sky is not going to make me settle down!'

Brando Marshall's loud protest down the phone to his sister was simultaneously heartfelt and indignant. 'What part of "I don't do relationships" don't you understand Bryony?' Not that he was about to enlighten her, but as far as women went he had three rules: plenty of them, never at home, and no repeats, although recently he'd put business before sex too often. He raked his fingers through his hair, shuddering at the fleetingly awful thought that Bryony might have any idea of the hard, hot sex he enjoyed, or worse, the hard, hot women he enjoyed it with. Slamming a mental door on that one, quickly, he shook his head at the realisation that this time she'd almost out-witted him. He could already feel the vibrations of the approaching helicopter.

'I'm only going to say this once, Bry! Regardless of what your motor-mouthed TV presenter boss with the hideous pink lips might have told the nation, I do *not* need a wife! And if I did, I certainly wouldn't be hooking up with some fortune-seeking low-life who writes in to some down-market TV show!'

'Okay. Take a chill pill Brando...'

One vault took him over the sofa and to the window. He peered at the lawn in front of the house, scrutinising the descending helicopter through a flurry of leaves, as it nudged to the ground.

Damned cheek of the girl! Bryony was only flying the woman in, using his *chopper!*

His face cracked into a slow smile. *Giving him the perfect means of escape.*

He vaulted over the sofa, and grabbed the phone again.

'Nice of you to borrow my helicopter without asking, but handy – I'm out of here! I'm off back to London right now, and you can get rid of the woman...'

He was going with the split-second decision.

Belting along the landing, he halted for a nano-second as he reached the top of the stairs. He knew the staff went apoplectic when he did his parkour moves around the house, but what the hell? He wouldn't be around to catch the fall out. He bent his knees, and flung himself into the air.

Whoosh. Nothing like the rush of carved balusters and deep pile carpet spinning past your face at forty miles an hour.

Three flick-flacks, an equal number of thumps and groans from ancient timbers, and he was streaking across the hall, only stopping to hurl open the huge front door.

Tearing wind slapped him head-on as he dashed into the late October cold, his t-shirt flapping wildly. With one leap, he'd cleared the stone steps outside the front door, then the gravel crunched beneath his converse as he sped on towards the grass. He pulled to a halt as he saw a figure alight from the helicopter. Someone slight, bending down now, waving their arms, holding onto their flapping jacket. A woman.

The woman.

Struggling.

He grimaced. She straightened to standing and he got a view as she spun. He clocked a suit and hair pinned back securely enough to resist the turbulence. A cabin bag-on-wheels.

'Damn you Bryony!' He was muttering under his breath now. 'Why the hell have you sent an air hostess?'

He took in endless legs, heels, a nipped-in waist. His eyebrows shot upwards in immediate appreciation, and he heard himself let out a long, low whistle, with no apparent input on his part.

And wow, she was stacked. An air hostess, who was stacked!

Quick re-assessment. 'Nice work, Bryony!'

But he was still out of here.

He dragged himself back to the scene unfolding in front of him, in apparent slow-motion. The air hostess turned. Huge black glasses, dwarfing a delicate face, took him by surprise, then a smile at least as wide as the Atlantic whacked him somewhere in the solar plexus, and surprised him some more. He felt his hand rise and he gave himself a mental kick as he realised he was waving to her. She lifted her hand off her thigh, and gave an enthusiastic wave in return.

For crazy sakes don't grin at her you fool!

The last thing he needed to look was welcoming, dammit.

She held her hand aloft, as if she were waiting for his smile before she let it fall, but Brando had stopped thinking about smiling, and instead had his eyes fixed on the hemline of her skirt, flirting in the buffeting wind.

Bingo!

A freak gust tore at the pleats and blasted them skywards. Before she had time to react, the air hostess skirt had twisted inside out, and was billowing, wildly, somewhere around her ears.

'Nice one!'

Brando's face cracked into an involuntary smile. Just what a guy needed to brighten a dreary afternoon. Maybe there was a god after all. Stocking tops, delicious dark knickers, he had enough time to make out the pattern of the lace. He gave a nod of appraisal.

'Twelve out of ten for that bottom – at the very least.'

A tug at the base of Brando's stomach, and a constriction of denim in the groin area, indicated that the skirt wasn't all that was rising.

Resist the urge to help a damsel in distress.

Given he would be leaving as-soon-as, there was no point in complicating the issue. He looked away. Next time he looked she was bent double, her arms wrapped around her knees, skirt firmly in place, feet solidly planted, but her body was gyrating.

She almost looked as though her feet were...

It took two blinks for Brando to know she was about to lose her balance, and one more for him to shoot across the grass, and grab hold of her before she crashed to the ground.

'Watch out!'

It was a shout, but the helicopter blades spun his words away.

The fact that he'd ended up cradling her bottom in his crotch was incidental. The important thing was he had saved her the embarrassment of a face-plant. Her body jack-knifed against him, stiffened, then the warmth of her soft buttocks passed straight through her skirt pleats, and set his groin on fire.

'Sorry about...'

Damn. Now he was pulling her onto a huge hard-on, and the fact that he could feel her breasts folding onto his hands somewhere round her front was making matters worse. From the vibrations in her torso, she was obviously saying something. Still grasping her tightly he pressed his ear closer to her mouth, struggling to hear what she said over the roar of the engines. He was rewarded with a brush with a pillow-soft cheek, and a spiky jab in the eye from her specs.

'What are you playing at?'

Was that what she was saying?

He couldn't be sure. He tried to disentangle himself, but felt her lean into him. What the hell? She was pointing to her feet now, twisting, gesticulating, shouting words he still failed to grasp.

He looked down.

Lots of mud, all over her shoes. And those surely had to be eff-me shoes, if ever he'd seen them. And right this moment, his blood was all heading one place, making damn sure he was ready to oblige. *Yes Siree!*

He needed to get a grip here. A grip of the situation, rather than the woman would be useful. It took a moment to disengage his brain from his libido, then it hit him.

'You're stuck?'

She grimaced at him, stuck fast and unable to move with both hooker-high heels firmly impaled in his lawn.

Through the huge lenses of her glasses, her panicky eyes were smoky purple. And she smelled of summer. That was it. Summer.

Summer and sex.

'Hang on to me!'

He dipped down, shivered as her hands closed around his head to steady herself, then he prised one foot at a time out of her shoes.

And not just any sex, hot sex.

His libido thrust into overdrive, and once more he made a valiant attempt to disengage it, as he wrenched her shoes out of the ground, stood up fast, and rammed them into her hand.

'I'm just leaving...' He was yelling, but she shrugged back at him.

Jeez, he'd come here to get in the chopper, get the hell out of here, or better still, to wave the woman back to wherever she'd flown in from. So why wasn't he pressing ahead and doing just that? He blinked away the miniscule twitch in his left eye. That tiny giveaway. His unfailing, gut-fuelled instinct kicked in.

'Looks like this is the only way...'

As he bent his knees, braced himself, and grasped hold of his air hostess, he saw her eyes go bright with surprise.

When the hell had she become his *air hostess?*

Up close now, he clocked the strawberry curve of her lips as they parted in astonished protest, and knew he was on the right track. He swung her easily into his arms, and turned, and strode towards the house, with his jaw set. Whatever was happening to him, he was determined to shake it off fast.

11

Feet dangling.

Cheek rammed unceremoniously against the rocky shoulder of a man who smelled delectable, and seemed in no hurry to put her down.

Not quite how Shea had planned her entrance to Edgerton Manor.

Her heart was still pounding from the shock of being literally swept off her feet, but at least that had solved the immediate problem of how to cross the sea of mud and reach the house without damaging her shoes further.

'You can put me down now, thanks.'

For a fleeting moment she was dizzied by the whole male proximity thing. She'd almost forgotten how it felt. Come to think of it, she'd *never* been man-handled like this. There was something appalling about the raw thrill vibrating through her. She didn't have herself down as a sucker for caveman tactics.

'I said you can put me down!'

She forced her eyes beyond the line of the sensuously stubbled jaw inches above her face, and caught a view of a ceiling as high as the sky, and the twinkliest chandelier she'd ever seen. When she looked back again, he was motionless, staring down at her, and her gaze locked onto slate-hard grey eyes and a quizzical smirk that made her stomach flip.

'If you insist on putting your head in the wolf's mouth, you can expect to get bitten!' His growl was rough as bitter chocolate. 'Your choice. Don't say I didn't warn you!'

Before she had time to work out what he meant by that, the world swung, and he lowered her legs, setting her down gently. Then backed away.

So much for keeping a professional distance.

Shea wriggled, took a minute to wrestle her crumpled jacket into approximately the right places, smooth her box-pleats into order. Muddy feet, or muddy shoes? She went with the stilettos, and gained the immediate five inch boost she needed.

'That's more like it!'

She flicked a tentative smile at the guy who had retreated a pace or two, but was still watching her with chilling determination, a large dose of disdain and an even larger dose of mental undressing. And the way his eyes locked onto her boobs brought her nipples out to graze the inside of her bra cups. She gave a shudder, as she looked back at him. Her eyes took in a broken-down t-shirt which she already knew covered the hardest of bodies, jeans ripped through in places, and low-slung, pretty much to the point of indecency. She pulled herself up sharply for letting her gaze linger a second too long on the most indecent bit, chided herself for the shiver rush that zinged down her spine when she took in the size of things in that area, becoming more defined by the moment. She shuddered again when she remembered she might be slightly responsible for that.

Crikey! Shea didn't know where this lusty inner woman had appeared from, but she needed to be slapped back into line, and fast.

'And what an amazing chandelier!'

She flipped a random space-filler comment, and a sparkly smile in his direction, hoping to nudge a response, as she assessed him. Way too good looking for his own good, and everyone else's, not that his threadbare appearance fooled her. Not only was there the flagrant mental undressing thing going on, but there was a super-arrogance to his swagger, the kind of major, understated confidence, that was only ever claimed by hugely successful men. Whatever promises had been made to her about his absence, the vagabond who studied her now, with that mix of veiled animosity and contempt, not to mention the double dose of white heat, had to be Brando Marshall.

So. Now she had the measure of him – to be handled with extreme care, keeping boobs and bottom out of his sightline if at all possible – she could afford to introduce herself. Let's face it, someone had to make the first move here, and it didn't look as if it was going to be him.

'Hi, I'm Shea. Shea Summers.'

She checked the brightness of her smile, extended a slim hand towards him, giving it a little rub in passing to make sure she'd got the mud off.

He tilted his head slightly, slid those dark-lashed, lingering eyes off her chest, and up to her face. And dammit for the way that made her stomach lurch. But otherwise he didn't move.

A strange confidence, founded on familiarity, was seeping through her, filling her with warmth and strength.

Wealthy, and reluctant?

Brilliant. Something she encountered on a daily basis, apart from the flagrant sexuality obviously, which frankly she couldn't remember meeting anything like, ever. Dealing with that disarming and alarming trait was something she's have to think about hard. Later. A lot later. But she'd cut her teeth on stroppy Manchester footballers, regularly won over billionaires who had more attitude than sense, loved nothing more than the challenge of a recalcitrant businessman. Here was someone she could handle without a problem. In theory. So long as she got his out of control libido into line. She noted the sullen curl of his far too sensuous lip, and couldn't help smiling more. Stamping on the tiny part of her brain that asked what it would feel like to be snogged by a guy with a mouth like that, she wondered where the hell her professionalism had gone. Probably left beside the helicopter, along with her self-respect, when she got dragged off by a caveman.

'I'm Shea,' she carried on, infusing her voice with a cheery ring of confidence, 'that's S-H-E-A, as in day. And I'm here to help!'

She could hardly keep the laughter out of her voice now, as she noted his left eyebrow arch in surprise above his deepening scowl. She readjusted her expression to hide her delight. Boy, was she going to have fun here. She gave her mouth-obsessed brain another sharp kick. It was all too much to keep in line here; this guy, his illegal body, not to mention her own totally out of character reactions.

He leaned nonchalantly on the elegantly turned newel post at the bottom of the expansive staircase now, rubbing a thumb absently across his chin. Quite why that made her think of stubble rubbing across the tender skin of her inner thigh was beyond her. At least he couldn't see her thought bubbles, although from the way he was scrutinising her, she couldn't be one hundred percent sure of that. When he made no move to greet her, she forced herself to push on, airily.

'You're Brando, I presume? I'm sure we'll be seeing a lot more of each other in the next few days.'

She waited, watching to see his reaction, and saw a wicked grin spread across his face, obliterating all traces of bad temper, simultaneously doubling up on the lust. 'Whatever you say, Miss S-H-E-A-rhymes-with-day! I'll look forward to that, very much, especially bearing in mind that some of us have seen quite a lot already, by way of a preview!'

His left eyebrow shot up, and he gave her a meaningful nod, and another blast of undiluted lust. Men who were this hot shouldn't be allowed out in public. She was usually impervious, but this was something else.

Shea felt the flush burn across her cheeks as she mentally rewound, flashed back to see her skirt flapping around her elbows. *Damn.* She'd walked into that one.

She whipped her brain into gear, searching desperately for a snappy reply, but before she'd found one, he'd sprung forward, and seized her hand, his strong, broad fingers wrapping around her own for a second.

'No worries!' His hand landed on her arm for a fleeting, searing moment. 'What's a stocking top between friends, after all?' His grin had spread, and he was laughing now, showing beautiful, not-quite-perfect teeth, but along with the laughter there was something else brooding in those dark, sooty eyes.

Shea reeled, as she took in the smoulder. Pure unadulterated desire, if ever she'd seen it, oozing, from each and every delectably rugged pore. Then she reeled again, as an electric aftershock zigzagged up her arm where he'd touched her hand.

'So, I'm here to...' Before she could claw herself out of the cavernous hole she was in, he interjected.

'We all know why you're here.' He sounded almost belligerent now. 'I wasn't sure you were going to be needed, but given what I've seen thus far, I'll make an exception. That's if you're up for a couple of days of play before you leave?'

The way he growled the word *play* sent a shower of anticipation down her spine. Anticipation? She wasn't an anticipator, dammit, because she didn't participate. Full stop. In fact the merest thought of participating sent an undertow of guilt to tug at her stomach. So what the heck was going on? Something in the way he narrowed his eyes as he waited for her reaction, told her he was pushing her. She blocked out the messages in her brain that were urging her, or rather commanding her, to hurl her body straight into his arms. Instead she watched him carefully, sizing up the opponent, knowing he'd already twisted this into some sort of game. One she wasn't completely sure she was winning right now.

'So, let's get this straight. I'm here to tidy – tidy and organise. That's all. And from what I hear there's a lot to go at. As I understand it, that's what I've been engaged to do...' She noted the tiniest flinch of his cheek as he heard the word 'engaged.'

Perhaps it was that flinch, that miniscule indication of weakness that made her do what she did next. That, combined with her instinct for reading difficult men, and her ability to bring them, whimpering, to heel, in record time. Mr Intense Hunk here was so far outside her experience she didn't feel confident to lump him in that manageable category, but whatever, there was no other explanation for what happened next. She heard her voice, loud, confident, and resonant, echoing around the hallway before she even knew she was going to speak.

'And of course, I'm also here to try out to be your wife!'

Where that lie had come from, she had no idea.

Wham!

She watched in triumph as his face jack-knifed as he heard the word 'wife.'

And she'd got him! That was the body blow. Manageable after all, perhaps. Phew! She'd located his Achilles heel in record time, though it hadn't been difficult, given it was one shared by most of the other thirty-something males she'd come across in his socio-economic bracket.

So, the man was entirely allergic to the idea of a wife, was he?

This suited her perfectly, given that the last thing she was looking for was a husband. She relished the power this scrap of insight gave her. It was useful ammunition, should she need to defend herself. But best of all, goading him gently was going to be very enjoyable.

Bring on the fun!

She rubbed her cheek, adjusted her glasses, and tried to hide her smile, as she waited for his reaction.

'Mrs McCaul! Come and meet Shea.'

Shea jumped at his unexpectedly hearty shout. Beyond him a straight woman with a softening smile was coming towards her, pulling a briefcase on wheels.

'Mrs McCaul is our housekeeper here at Edgerton.' The curl of his lip suggested that he would have happily added 'and resident pain in the behind,' as he extended his arm in a half-hearted presentation.

'Shea rhymes-with-roll-in-the-hay Summers, meet Mrs McCaul. Shea, by the way, is hell-bent on finding herself a husband, and has apparently set her heart on a spot of gold-digging here at Edgerton.' He flashed a mocking look at Shea, who inwardly shrank at this blistering introduction, but held her head high.

Mrs McCaul whisked past Brando, shaking her head, and

handed Shea the case with a solid smile.

'Don't listen to him, Shea, we know what you're here for, and everything's ready for you in the annex, as Bryony asked. So if you'd like to follow me...'

Mrs McCaul's lilting Scottish tones lapped over Shea, as she rifled through her handbag, shed her stilettos, pulled out a pair of brown suede pumps, and slipped them on.

'Not so fast!' Brando's voice was biting now. 'Shea will be staying in the Snowfield Wing with me. No arguments.'

'But...' The women's protests chimed together, but Brando chopped them short.

'Didn't you hear, I said 'No arguments!' If you want to stay at all, Shea, this is how it's going to be. It's non-negotiable. There's plenty of space up there.' He shot her a smirking *that'll teach you* look. 'No point coming to hook a husband, then hiding away from him, is there?'

Shea blanked the shiver his look sent down her back, and opened her mouth to reply – not that she had decided what to say – but found there was no chance of chipping into the battle hotting up before her.

'Very well, Brando. Luckily for us, you're not here often, with manners like that!' Mrs McCaul jutted her chin at him. 'You should take lessons from your sister. Bryony may be younger, but she's the perfect lady!'

Wow! Shea clocked Brando's silent grimace. One big revelation there! Bryony was more than just the TV girl. That explained a lot.

Mrs McCaul dismissed Brando with a snort, though as she turned, Shea caught a long-suffering twinkle of affection in her eyes. 'Don't worry Shea, he won't be bothering you for long. He rarely graces us with his presence for more than one night at a time, so he's already well overdue to leave.'

'Thanks for sharing that, Mrs McCaul.' His tone was caustic. 'I'll show Shea up to her room myself now. By the way, we'll be having supper in the west wing dining room later, if that's okay

18

with you. I take it you'll have time to remove the dust sheets.'

Mrs McCaul looked perturbed. 'Perhaps not the best choice Brando. You'd be much more comfortable eating in the kitchen, as you usually do. That dining room is very...'

He cut in abruptly. 'Very whatever! It's my choice, and that's where we'll be eating, thank you!'

Shea heard the polished oak boards creak gently as Brando turned and sauntered casually towards the staircase.

Wow! Rear of the year, or what? She let out a silent gasp of appreciation. Not that she was in the least bit interested, but a view like that could hardly go un-applauded.

'Shoes, Brando!'

Mrs McCaul's curt instruction flew after them, and Shea stood open mouthed and watched as Brando kicked off first one then the other sneaker, flipped them, and nonchalantly caught them as he walked.

'Are you coming or am I going to have to wait all day?' He was calling to her impatiently over his shoulder now, already halfway up the stairs, mounting them three at a time.

Shea wavered, chewing her thumbnail and not entirely sure what she was doing. She'd come in feet first, feeling thoroughly shaken, and even more thoroughly stirred. And she didn't *do* stirred. Never. Brando was the rudest guy she'd met, and he wasn't even supposed to be here. And now she was following this commitment-phobe up to his 'wing,' when he obviously saw her as some money-grubbing opportunist, who he was determined to wipe the floor with.

And just five minutes ago she'd thought this was a walkover.

'If you don't come now I can guarantee you'll get lost, and I won't be responsible if the wolf gets you!'

His gravelly words spiralled down from the landing, and sent goosebumps down her spine...

And what the heck was all this about wolves anyway?

All a million miles away from what she'd been expecting. But then...

19

'I can always come back and carry you.'

Glancing up, she saw him watching her coolly over the balustrade, eyes narrowed and calculating, poised for action.

Cripes, he wasn't joking either.

Grabbing her muddy shoes in one hand, and her bag in the other, she bolted towards the stairs.

Chapter Two

'It's eight thirty pm, I hope you're ready!'

Brando's shout outside Shea's door was loud enough to make the handle rattle, and it matched his mood.

Ready? Who was he kidding? When had a woman ever been ready?

He'd spent the remainder of the afternoon fuming. Fuming with Bryony for landing him in this situation, and fuming with this damned woman who'd helicoptered her way into his private domain. After years in the music business, he reckoned he was unshockable. But what kind of woman would be pushy enough to pull a stunt like this to grab a husband? And what the hell had he been thinking to go along with it? He must have had some kind of consciousness blackout.

He let out one disgusted snort, and raised his hand to add a knock, but before his knuckle made contact, the door flew open.

Bang. Hot sweet woman. His head reeled as her scent hit him full on.

'Absolutely ready Brando! Or I will be in two minutes...'

So he was right. Of course she wasn't ready!

He leaned on the doorframe, and drummed his fingers idly, as she spun back into the room. Took in a shapely little black dress. No sleeves. A brave choice at Edgerton, in late October. High, high heels. And black lace stockings that made the backs of her calves look delectable as she walked away from him, then propelled his libido into the stratosphere as she knelt down in front of the fireplace. Yanking his lust firmly into line, he noticed that whatever the fire in his groin was doing, the fire in the grate wasn't blazing.

'I'd better help with that. Much as you need to learn about the rigors of life in a stately home, I'd hate you to be cold tonight.' As he strode over, he caught the chestnut glint in her swept-up hair, then the exposed nape of her neck, as she bent over the hearth.

White and vulnerable. His gut gave a twist of guilt at the thought of using and dispatching her. Except she'd walked into this, dammit, and hell, he knew better than to be taken in by downy napes of necks. This woman was here to play for high stakes. A swift dispatch was nothing less than she deserved, and if a tumble in the manorial bed was what was needed to achieve that, he was more than willing to go down that road, but the more he saw of those curves, the hotter that end game was shaping up to be.

As he knelt down next to her by the fire, he let his thigh bump lightly against hers. She jerked away from him, and the poker she was holding clattered onto the hearth.

Jumpy or what?

Picking up the poker, he riddled the embers back to life energetically. He knew Mrs McCaul always checked the fires, but what the heck? It was worth it, for the tease – and the insanely sexy blast of lace stretched taut across Shea's knees. Perhaps his judgement hadn't been so clouded after all. The promise of what was to come was looking sweeter by the second.

'Thanks for helping with that! I'm not used to coal fires. I'll just get my phone.' She stood up, and the grateful smile she flashed down at him as she unfolded those glorious legs sent his stomach into a crazy freefall for the second time that day. He regularly threw his body through corkscrew twists and flips, but hauling Shea Summers into the house earlier that day had sent his insides spinning like never before. And now it had happened

22

again, dammit.

'Forget your phone. There's no signal at all here. Another of the wonders of Edgerton! Are you coming then?' he snapped, before he jumped up, marched through the doorway, and strode off down the landing.

No way was he looking back. The floorboards, creaking under her uneven high-heeled lurches, told him she was following closely behind, and he only slowed as he reached the dining room door. As he threw it open, stepping back to let her pass, a freezing gale slammed him in the face. Ha! Just as he'd expected. Despite the roaring fire, the lofty room was bitterly cold and inhospitable. Miss Shea made-in-a-day Summers was about to experience the full glory of the west dining room.

'Come on in! I see you lost the glasses then!'

He'd noticed in her bedroom, but the full effect floored him now, as he saw her head-on. High cheekbones, gently turned-up nose, and the fullest lips. *Disarmingly pretty.* Very different without the big frames. He'd had her down as pushing thirty, but now, despite the confident jut of her chin, he doubted she was even twenty five.

She skimmed past him into the room, and he heard her gasp as the cold hit her, saw pale goosebumps springing out on her arms as he moved to pull out a heavy mahogany chair for her. Across the white damask tablecloth the candle flames stuttered in the draught, and suddenly, showing her the uncomfortable reality of life in a stately pile was starting to feel like poor judgement. Arriving opposite her, he got the full effect of her ample chest complete with erect nipples, sticking prominently through the thin fabric of her dress, no doubt whipped to attention by the chill.

Double jeopardy.

Definitely a bad call. He felt his blood surge south. *Damn.* He was in for an uncomfortable evening all round.

'If you don't mind, I think I'll just go and get something warmer...' She'd gone before he had time to reply, and when she returned she had added a sharp tailored jacket. Marks out of ten for passion killers? He'd give an eleven. At least that sorted the immediate too-exciting nipple problem.

'Desperate times call for desperate measures, and all that!' She flashed violet eyes at him, and something in their mocking glint told Brando she was ahead of his game. 'Sorry about the style clash, but I haven't brought my arctic gear with me. I'd have taken the time to put jeans on, but we wouldn't want dinner to get cold, would we?'

Back in the room, and looking like someone from a head office boardroom, complete with an identity name-tag hanging from her lapel.

'You really haven't brought anything warmer with you?' He watched in disbelief as she shook her head. What kind of numbskull would rock up to a draughty hole like Edgerton without so much as a sweater?

'Nope. Sorry. I'm a central heating girl, and I wasn't expecting glacial, so you're stuck with me in my O 4 Organise work gear.'

'I'll go and find you something more...' He left the room before bothering to finish.

Suitable, hot, sexy? Warm maybe?

Any of the above – he wasn't fussy. Sure, he didn't want her here, and yes, he did suspect her motives, but hell, he wasn't completely heartless. He'd meant for her to understand that country houses weren't always luxurious, not for her to catch pneumonia. As for what the whole O-4 thing was all about, he was still praying she wasn't some high powered dominatrix when he came back moments later, and dropped two cashmere sweaters in her lap.

'There you go, Madame Chairman, they're mine, but they're warmer than anything else you've got here. Put them on, and tell me what the heck O 4 Organise is.' He watched intently as she peeled away her jacket, and pulled on his own jumpers. How could she look so sexy wearing two men's sweaters?

'Thanks, that's much better.' She was rolling the sleeves back now, pushing dislodged pins back into her hair. 'O 4 Organise is the exclusive personal organising company I work for. I run the Manchester end. I thought I was going to be able to put my expertise to good use here, but to be honest it all looks a lot less chaotic than the shots I saw on the programme.'

He had a vague memory of the TV crew deliberately trashing the annexe to get the shots they needed, when views of endless rooms under dust sheets had failed to excite them.

'Never believe what you see on TV.' He spat the words out with a rueful shake of his head.

'But Bryony said...'

He jumped in and cut her short. 'Rule One when dealing with Bryony: Never believe what she says.' Then he kicked himself for not waiting to hear exactly what Bryony *had* said. No doubt it would make for interesting listening, and he may well have asked, but just then, Mrs McCaul arrived with dinner.

Brando dug into the steaming beef stew and dumplings with gusto, hoping to mask his unease. He usually ate on the hoof, snatching a sandwich in the office, or grabbing a takeaway in front of the TV. Formal meals didn't figure on his agenda, and he *never* ate with women. Strawberries and liquid chocolate consumed from a platter of bare flesh aside, if he was with a woman it was for sex, not food. So the double assault on his system, of Mrs McCaul's substantial supper and a hot woman eating opposite him, was throwing him off. Between forkfuls he tried to decide if Shea was mentally undressing him with those scathing looks of hers, or simply trying to peer into his soul.

It was some time, and a lot of stew later, when she finally struck up meaningful conversation. 'So where in Scotland are we exactly?'

Brando gave her a hard stare. 'Who told you Edgerton was in Scotland?'

'I'm not sure, didn't it say that on the programme?' She hesitated, her fork halfway to that delectable mouth of hers.

'There you go, what did I say about not believing everything

25

you hear on TV?' He gave a snort of laughter. 'To be fair, they did keep the location a secret, but I'm damned sure no-one said anything about Scotland. The only Scottish thing about here is Mrs McCaul and her full-on Edinburgh accent!'

'Okay...' He watched Shea's eyes widen, then her brows furrowed as she processed this nugget. 'So where are we then?'

'Classified information here, I hope you can be trusted. Edgerton is in the Cotswolds.' He bit back his smile as he tried to contain his laughter.

'Sorry. Not helpful.' She shook her head and looked blank. 'You'll have to be more specific. *Cotswolds* doesn't mean anything to me. Where's it near?'

This he found hard to believe. Had to be a wind-up, but he'd play along. 'Cirencester, Cheltenham, Gloucester?' She still looked blank. He'd try something easier. 'Oxford?'

She thought hard, scrunched her lip, shook her head. 'Still not helpful. Maybe if I saw it on a map?'

Brando stopped chewing, put down his knife and fork. This he found hard to believe.

'What?' Shea's shriek was high and defensive. 'So! I don't have the geography gene! I can't help it! I don't know where anywhere is, unless I've been there, if I don't see it on a map. We can't all be perfect and know everything. I don't have the history gene either come to that, but there are a lot of things I can do, and do very well, so back off!'

So Shea-what-do-you-say might have a great ass, but she didn't have the first clue where she was, and what's more she wasn't trying to hide the fact, nor did she feel the need to apologise. Interesting combination. And boy did she look feisty when she did angry!

She lowered her eyes for a second, and when she looked up at him again it was with a half smile that spread to a wide grin. 'When you warned me about getting lost in the house earlier, you were closer to the mark than you thought!'

Zap!

26

That smile caught him off guard, and smacked him square in the stomach.

'I think we've done enough dining room penance for one day. I'll get Mrs McCaul to serve pudding by the fire in my sitting room, and I'll show you a map. We'll be much cosier there.'

Jeez, had he really just said that!

He asked himself a) where that had come from and b) why the heck he'd used the word *cosy*. He never said cosy! It was like someone else was operating his mouth. *Jeez again!* He needed to stop panicking, remember this was his infallible instinct, working to push the situation to a quick conclusion. Hell, a frosty dining room was hardly conducive to the moves he had in mind, and he was aiming to get this whole thing over at break-neck speed. And there was something else he'd noticed. Sure this Shea was sexy enough, with her curves and lively nipples and splashy smiles, but he'd seen the way she flinched when he came anywhere near her, and he'd sensed a curious pent-up tension. Uptight didn't begin to cover it. A quick tumble in the sack with a man with his taste for wild and wicked was just what was needed to send this woman running for the hills. See her off for good. Job done.

A sudden crush in his groin suggested his libido was in definite agreement.

* * *

Peach cobbler, egg custard, coffee and liqueurs. All in the comfort of the boss's private sitting room. Cosy was his way of describing it. Too damned intimate was hers.

Shea wondered how she'd let it happen, which part of her active mind hadn't been functioning. She could only blame the cold for her brain freeze.

Pudding in the snug would have been beyond the limit of her professional boundaries at the best of times. But peering over maps in flickering firelight, with a hunk who set her heart banging horribly every time his arm stretched across and grazed hers? That was in the way-out-of line category. Just the memory of it was enough to make her cringe with guilt. Thank goodness she'd had the sense to make a quick exit.

Back in the safe haven of her room, she stripped off her dress, dragged some shorts over her tights, and slipped one of the borrowed sweaters over her bra, definitely not because it smelled of raw man she assured herself, but because after an hour of wearing it, she was completely addicted to the softness and the warmth. As she pulled the pins out of her hair and dragged her curls into submission, she noticed her useless mobile on the coffee table. A phone call with her mum wasn't going to happen tonight. No bad thing. She needed time to work out what the heck was going on here.

It wasn't so much *what* she'd been doing, but how she was reacting. It should have been completely possible to have got through this evening in a detached, professional manner. Her work constantly put her into intimate environments with men. She regularly marched in, pulled some guy's bedroom to pieces, put it all together again, and marched right on out. She'd always assumed her ability to freeze advances before they'd even happened was because of her past hanging around her like an invisible force field. That coupled with her 'no-nonsense' attitude. She'd worked alongside a whole bunch of clients with less than perfect reputations and had always sailed through unscathed.

Until now.

Which was why she knew the fault here was completely her own.

She'd never been remotely attracted to anyone she'd worked for before, and she'd worked for some very attractive men. But there was a world of difference between recognising that someone was hot, and the full-blown force of attraction itself. And right here it was full-blown force. And she needed to get a grip. Quickly.

Brando Marshall might be good looking, but in every other aspect he was a total nightmare – bad tempered, rude, arrogant, treating his long-term employees with very little respect, and he obviously despised her... Quite a list. Any attraction to him was wrong, wrong, wrong, not to mention crazy. Lucky she'd got a handle on it from the start. Now all she had to do was stamp it out. Starting now.

A sudden rap on her door jolted her to her feet, and set her heart pounding.

'Shea, your mother's on the landline for you!' Brando's voice rose gruffly over his knock, and sent her stomach into a cartwheel. 'Take it in my sitting room, or my office if you prefer.'

Damn.

She hadn't thought her mum would ring tonight, or that she'd be back in the lion's den so soon, putting her new resolve to the test.

'Mothers, who'd have them? Sorry about this!' She shot him an apologetic grimace.

If she went at break-neck pace, if she didn't look at him, didn't stop, there wouldn't be time for anything misplaced or wrong. She threw open the door, whipped past an open-mouthed Brando, and bolted into his sitting room. 'My mum must be worried that she can't get through on my mobile and...'

Damn. She'd got ahead of him here. Now where should she go?

'Straight on...' He arrived behind her, close enough to engulf her with that dangerously delicious scent she so shouldn't be noticing, and waved an arm towards an open door on the other side of the room, beyond the sofas. She shot through it, and screeched to a halt.

Pink shrimps! She was in his bedroom!

Her heart did a double flip. She'd seen some imposing beds in her time but this one took the biscuit. She tried to ignore how inviting it looked.

His voice came from behind her now '...straight on to the office – the phone's on the desk.'

Could have been worse. She slammed up to the desk, and grasped the receiver. At least he wasn't in the bed.

Brando stood in the sitting room, raking his hands through his hair, watching the minutes tick by on his Rolex. How could a phone conversation with a mother could take so long? Hell, he'd have sat down if he'd realised. He tried to remember the last time he'd spoken to his own mother, and failed. All he needed to say had been said years ago, and none of it good. No need to revisit that one. He hauled himself back to the present again, as the creaking floor suggested Shea was finally about to emerge from the bedroom.

'Welcome back to the land of the living! Your mother must be a riveting conversationalist – remind me to say 'Hi' to her sometime when I've got a free day or two!'

She was hurtling towards him with a scared-rabbit look on her face and her legs a blur.

He hadn't noticed the detail as she'd flashed past him earlier, but he'd caught enough lace and thigh to make his pulse pound, and he moved to catch a full-frontal view.

Oh man!

How the hell had he missed that? He was going to miss it again if he didn't move, given that she was hurling herself at the door.

'Not so fast.' One swift sidestep, and he'd cut off her escape. Her sweet scent wafted around him as she pulled to a halt, narrowly avoiding landing on his toes. He felt his lips stretch into a broad, unscheduled smile, as he took in the long, curvy lace-covered legs rising to a scant inch of shorts showing below his pale grey sweater. And his lips weren't the only thing stretching here. With an almighty effort he screwed his smile from ecstatic to sardonic, and watched her push a tangle of hair out of her eyes, grab the v-neck that was sliding way beyond an already exposed shoulder, and turn on him with a wonderfully defiant pout.

This girl was good. Brazen even. Out for what she could get, and not scared to grab it. On principle, he despised her for the grasping audacity that had brought her here, but right now, there was something in her blatant ambition he had to admire. What he had to do next would be so much more enjoyable if he was dealing with an opponent who could hold her own. He liked to play hard-ball, and this girl looked like she'd be whacking them back. Shea Summers had put herself in his firing line and he was going to take her down, fighting and resisting. All the more fun.

He let his eyes play on her breasts, as they pushed prominently through the gauze of cashmere. 'Are you wearing a bra under that?'

If he'd shocked her with his direct question she didn't let on. She hesitated, but only for a second. Playing for time, perhaps?

'That's for me to know and you to find out.'

Nice reply. Batted straight back. That was good. He bit his lip hard, to distract himself from the fact that in his head his teeth were already grazing those nipples. He watched her brush away a stray curl. She had him fixed with her violet eyes now, her head inclined slightly. Weighing him up? Perhaps. Challenging him? Definitely.

Nothing he liked more than a challenge.

'So I take it you'll be sleeping with me tonight.' Two firm rules going out of the window there, but what the hell, if it brought this to a close. He slid it out casually, then waited for the reaction. He couldn't hold in a last jibe. 'It's what you're here for, after all, isn't it?'

The purple of her eyes darkened to indigo.

'That's what *you* think.'

Her tone was defiant, but her amused smile took him aback. She almost sounded dismissive. Not bothered. He'd see about that!

'Going to all this trouble to try for the position of my wife? Surely the try-out has to start in the bedroom? No time like the present, so why not now?'

She gave a light shrug. 'Maybe I prefer to know more about a man before I sleep with him, even if he does own a whopping, country house!'

He let out a snort of surprise.

31

Was this a brush-off she was giving here, or was she simply playing hard to get? He couldn't be sure. The way he usually operated, involved him eyeballing a woman he wanted, and she was his. He played, and he caught. End of. Afterwards he discarded.

That was the way it was for him. He'd never known it any other way. Not since... he throttled that thought, fast. Enough to say that as far the last decade went, he'd surfed the double aphrodisiac of wealth and power to the max. This reluctance, this rebuff was new, and he baulked momentarily, before his confidence kicked back into play.

'You'll soon change your mind.' He narrowed his eyes and looked up and down every last explosive inch of her, his testosterone-fuelled growl low and husky. 'Give you a day or two, and I guarantee you'll be begging.' Let's face it, they usually would.

He flashed her an arrogant grin, and tried to ignore the fact that right now he was the one who felt like doing the begging. She'd thrown him off balance here, and he needed to regroup. Damn the woman, damn her soft inviting thighs, and those breasts he ached to bury himself in. What the hell was he thinking? He didn't do soft in any shape or form, either in his life, or in the women he chose. And he definitely didn't do begging. Dammit! It was so long since he'd been with a woman, he'd made himself vulnerable. He was heading for a long hard cold shower. Time to take himself in hand, in more ways than one. And then he'd have an endorphin-blasting rip over the rooftops.

'Begging? You think I'd beg?' Her voice, high with incredulity, scythed into his thoughts. She hit him with a polar stare, and her voice dropped to a derisory hiss. 'Don't count on it, mate. If you're thinking I'll beg, you're liable to have a long, lonely wait. Now if you'll please excuse me, I'd like to get back to my room!'

So that was his dismissal, for this evening at least. He was ready to go with that. He slid aside, flung the door open, and soaked up the view of her bum cheeks wiggling beneath his sweater, as she marched on past him, and across the corridor.

Just before she disappeared, she whipped around to face him, arching her back against her door, and sticking out her chest in a way that finally flashed his smouldering groin into pure naked flames. Somewhere beneath the curtain of chestnut hair, he caught a rosy flush in her cheeks. She shot him a dimpled yet defiant grin, then, with a jut of her chin, added one resonant, parting thought.

'I'm not even sure you're my type!'

And then she was gone.

Brando gave another choke of derision.

Hah! This coming from a woman who'd happily thrown herself at an unknown guy to bag a stately home and a loaded husband. Successful billionaire, with a manor house and an estate was exactly her type.

Never a man to forgo the last word, he waited. Long enough for her to be was sure he was finished. Only then did he put his mouth to her keyhole, and shout.

'Not your type, eh? I think we both know me and my bank balance are exactly what you're looking for.'

And then he stormed back to his sitting room, and slammed the door hard enough to make the chandelier jangle.

Damn. Had he just committed to the long game? What the hell had happened to his plans to leave?

* * *

Shea spread a large dollop of home-made raspberry jam on her toast next morning, and pinched herself one more time to make damn sure this was really happening as she sipped her coffee in front of the fire. Waking up this morning she was surprised at the sense of relief she felt that she'd finally got away. It was strange to think she'd almost missed it altogether. If she hadn't come home early that Sunday evening she wouldn't be here, and she probably wouldn't even have known about the existence of Edgerton Manor. So like her zany housemates to be obsessed with some weekend

TV show about country piles, so like them to be ridiculous enough to get out the glue and scissors and start making postcards of themselves in various states of wedding dress – and undress – just because the presenter they loved to hate suggested some guy on TV needed a wife. And how weird it was to think that guy was Brando Marshall. It was all very well throwing herself into her work, but there were times when she knew she missed out. And although this trip was work related she was pleased she'd dared to come, even though she'd seemed the least likely candidate out of all of her friends to be chosen. To her mind even Guy was more suitable than her. At least his card made claims to him having a pert bum, a frilly apron, and superb washing up prowess, and at the time she assumed the disclaimer she'd scrawled on hers would put her out of the running completely. Whereas in fact when Bryony from the TV company had contacted Shea, she hadn't seemed particularly bothered about the 'wife' part at all.

Rule one: never believe what Bryony says... Brando's words from last night echoed round her head. Brando Marshall. She sighed, rolled her eyes at the way he'd wormed his way back into her thoughts despite her best efforts to keep him out, then glanced at her watch. White mice! Eight o'clock, and still in her pyjamas? Nothing to be proud of there. Okay, her excuse was she hadn't had the best night's sleep, but as far as getting her professional head into order and putting Brando Marshall back in the feel-no-attraction-whatsoever camp where he belonged, she was doing well. Last night she'd even managed to walk through the man's bedroom without a qualm. Dashing through, hurtling back.

Doing every action incredibly fast around Brando had worked. She'd felt nothing. *Who was she kidding here?* Well, not quite nothing. But she had plans to work on that today. The point was, she was firmly back in control, of herself and the situation, which was exactly where Shea Summers always needed to be.

She'd mostly managed to stave off his rudest queries, and suggestions, obviously designed to shock her.

So I take it you'll be sleeping with me...

The words echoed in her brain. She was still appalled by the way they'd made her skin dance, the way they'd set her heart clattering on her ribs. The twangs of guilt about her reaction had been reverberating round her head all night. She still felt ashamed that in that moment, some dark and hidden part of her was desperate to agree.

He was pushing her; he had to be playing a game.

No stranger in their right mind would ask you outright if you were wearing a bra, unless they were goading you. But somehow the completely outrageous nature of his behaviour made him easier for her to handle. She'd finally got him nailed. He was back in her Easy-to-Manage box. And that was where she was going to keep him.

She took another bite of toast, and thought how strange it felt to begin the morning so calmly, even if the thought of what Brando might do today had her stomach fluttering. Unless she was doing one of her famous dawn starts, breakfast invariably involved slopped tea and half asleep housemates, and always an early morning chat with her mum.

As if on cue, she heard Brando, calling from the corridor.

'Mrs Summers, in the office on line one, for you Shea!'

Right. One sickening tummy flip later, and she'd go with the flow. This wasn't a problem.

She primed herself to move fast, and, once again, had the door open before he'd finished knocking.

'Nice PJs.' His low laugh bounced off the panelling down the landing.

She was ready to outdo any quip he threw at her. Not quite so ready for the goosebump rash, or the way he smelled so deliciously of man, though. She braced herself.

'Yep, they're Wonder Woman pyjamas, and before you ask, yes, I am wearing knickers underneath. Phone still in the same place?' She was already halfway to his sitting room, aware of

35

Brando standing gawping in her doorway, when she realised he was speaking, and she thudded to a halt.

'Help yourself to the phone, I'm off out. Bryony's been on already, says a film crew's on its way. I guess you'll know what she means by that?' He paused and raised one quizzical eyebrow.

Her stomach gave a telltale lurch.

Damn. She knew she shouldn't have stopped, definitely shouldn't have met his gaze. Although looking him in the eye was preferable to staring at him in the other place her eyes were invariably drawn to. Not that she made a habit of ogling men's groins, but his was particularly...

Particularly what? She shouldn't even be going there!

Attractive? Promising? Illegally sexy?

Yes to all of the above. *Riveting. And also entirely off limits.*

What *was* she thinking?

Her brain had been well-behaved when she was moving. If she didn't get going she'd have mentally undressed him before she knew it.

Damn. Too late.

The carpet pile spread beneath her bare toes as she propelled herself forwards into a gallop. 'Okay, great, thanks Brando! See you!'

Forward, as far as possible, as fast as possible.

Then she'd be okay.

Sour worms, there was his bed again!

Already made. Almost looking as if it hadn't been slept in, she decided as she flew by, heading towards the office.

His teasing tones echoed after her as she scuttled away.

'Give my love to your mother!'

* * *

In her immediate panic to flee from Brando, and fit in an early morning check-in with her mother, there'd been no time for

36

Shea to worry about the film crew, which turned out to be one understated guy called Pete, looking for a couple of shots, on his way to another location.

So much for the whole 'lights-camera-action' team she'd been fearing.

All he'd done was to point a large video camera at her for ten seconds whilst she pretended to sit and drink coffee over the remains of her breakfast tray. And now they were going down to the terrace to take a shot of her approaching the front door.

She looked out of the window to check the weather. Blustery, but dry, judging by the whirling leaves. A movement in the distance caught her eye; a figure, running through the parkland, seemingly hurling themselves at every tree, then flipping back over, and landing on their feet again.

The pure exuberance of it made her smile.

There was something mesmerising about the relentless repetition, and although she was supposed to be following Pete downstairs, she hung on to watch until the person disappeared from view behind a distant copse.

Hurrying down the gracious staircase, she sighed ruefully, still thinking of the bouncing figure, as she wound her scarf around her neck. How great must it be to feel happy and carefree enough to want to do that?

* * *

Brando cursed as his feet hit the gravel at the top of the drive.

He'd been out running for an hour now, had already done two hours before his very early breakfast, and he'd been throwing himself over roofs in the dark last night, yet he still felt no sense of release.

He never slept well. He'd long since given up the hell of sleepless tossing and turning in bed, getting by on snatched naps in the office chair, but last night he hadn't been able to sleep at all. What was it going to take to make him feel better? The sheer concentration and physical effort his free running took were usually enough to wipe out his tension within minutes. But he wasn't usually this hyped up.

Damn this country life.

Nothing wound him up like a day at Edgerton, but he didn't usually suffer this much. He suspected it had something to do with the blasted woman Bryony had dropped on him, but he certainly wasn't going to let a woman take credit for landing him in this state. Okay, he hadn't been able to get her out of his damned brain since he set eyes on her, but where women were concerned he was immune and untouchable. End of.

He approached the avenue of trees along the south drive. Sixty-three trees each side. He'd do all hundred-and-twenty-six of them. Somehow he doubted he'd feel unwound afterwards, but at least he'd achieve the oblivion of exhaustion.

He bounced on the balls of his feet.

Damn Shea Summers.

Then flung himself at the nearest tree trunk.

* * *

Seventy two trees in, sensing movement in front of the house, he broke his rhythm to pause, and watched two people emerge, then walk around in animated discussion.

Bingo, it was her!

Had to be. And a guy with a camera.

Without thinking, he veered off across the park towards them, sprinting over the grass. He prided himself on his low heart-rate, but right now his pulse was banging through his body. Springing up the steps onto the terrace, he vaulted over a wooden seat, and arrived beside the pair with a grin, his hands stuffed as far into the pockets of his low-slung jeans as he could reach.

'Nice morning for filming!'

Shea and the cameraman turned to include him now. He met Shea's glance, and gave a wide, unrepentant, laid-back grin. 'I hope you're wearing...'

But she was too fast for him. Before he could finish, she'd jumped in.

'Yes Brando, I do have underwear on.' She gave him a glib smirk. 'I'd ask if you do, but given that half your Y-fronts appear to be on public display already, the question seems unnecessary! Good to see you shop at Calvin Klein.'

Nice one! Who'd have thought Miss Frosty-morning would have had that in her.

Feisty he could deal with.

Her hair was scraped back and he found himself wanting to pull it free, shake it loose, bury his fingers in the strands.

'Pete just wants to get a shot of me walking into the house. It shouldn't take long and then we're done here.' She was speaking to him brusquely now, her elbows by her ears, as she fiddled to replace a pin at the back of her hair. He caught a blinder of her breasts as she spun around.

'Fine! Whatever you say,' he chortled, chewing his thumbnail absently, aware that his eyes had locked on target as if they'd been superglued. 'It's a bit chilly out here, even for cashmere. You may want to add some nipple shields before you do the final take, but then what do I know?'

Shea glanced down, swung her arms around herself quickly, then recovering with enviable speed, turned her back on him firmly.

'Not a problem, Pete's mostly filming my back in any case, so it seems you're the only one here worried by my nipple status.' She flashed him a smile over a carefully positioned shoulder. 'Shall we carry on, Pete?'

Blast. He shot himself in the foot there, now she'd be keeping her back to him for sure.

Yes Pete, no Pete. He gritted his teeth, and rocked on his heels as he watched her walk towards the door. Then she walked back, tilting her head towards that darned cameraman as they shared some joke, then she went again, this time shooting a smile over her shoulder as she disappeared into the house. Then she reappeared, and it looked like they had a wrap.

'You do realise this is all bull, don't you Pete?' Brando knew he was sounding belligerent now, but somehow he couldn't stop, and he didn't give a damn. 'It didn't happen like this at all. I know you guys aren't big on truth, but you might as well go one more time, and get close to what really happened.'

Brando stepped towards Shea, and had her scooped up, caught fast in his arms, before she had time to let out so much as a squawk. 'There you go, that's a lot more like what happened yesterday, if it's an action replay you're after.' He clasped her close to his chest. 'Shea Summers being carried over the threshold, I hope you're getting this Pete!'

Jeez, she felt soft...

With long steps, he strode across the terrace with her in his arms, her bottom bouncing all the way on his rapidly growing erection, pausing only to throw the door open. He bounded into the house, kicked the door, and it slammed resoundingly behind them.

Chapter Three

Time seemed to stand still in the echoing calm of the hall. Shea was lying, completely passive in his arms. He stole a glance down at her, and met her expression of long-suffering disgust.

'Well done, Brando. Great shot, which I'm sure the viewing public will no doubt appreciate. Now will you please put me down.' That was a fierce, no-messing command.

Suddenly reluctant to give up her warm yielding curves, he gripped her more tightly to him, took in the fullness of her mouth.

'No, as it happens, I'm not going to put you down!' He flashed her a defiant grin.

Not before he'd taught her a lesson.

As the pattern of his breathing broke, he felt the echo of a shudder pass through her. The slightest tremble of her bottom lip sent a twang through his chest.

Not before he'd had his fun.

No point delaying what had to be done. No point at all. He dragged her closer to his face, brought his mouth crashing down onto hers.

Wham-bam!

Not a shred of resistance! He slid straight through the strawberries-and-cream of lip gloss, and plunged to the sweetest, raspberry and vanilla depths. And, morning stars, she was not only letting

41

him in, she was kissing him back! Kissing him back, kissing him big, kissing him bravely and hard and hungrily.

Desperately hungrily.

He hadn't bargained for being belted practically into orbit, nor for being left hanging in some crazy airless free-fall, that progressed into a glorious, gyroscopic tumble. He had no idea how long he'd been kissing her, only that he never wanted it to end. Then a frenzied fist hammering on his head yanked him halfway back to earth.

'Brando! What the...' Shea's shriek hauled him the rest of the way back to reality. 'I said put me down, not eat my face!'

Remembering his manners now, he obligingly tilted her gently towards the floor, and set her down as neatly as his wobbling legs and gigantic erection would allow.

Wobbling legs? Since when had his legs ever wobbled?

Shea staggered backwards, and sent him a searing glare as she rearranged her sweater. The way she pulled at the hem to cover that flash of bare skin was delicious, and thunderously arousing every time, but sending his erection to places it shouldn't go. Dragging his belt higher, he attempted to stall the escape bid. No way should he be hanging round Shea Summers, and those luscious boobs of hers, in low slung jeans. She needed the nipple shields more than ever now, he noted with satisfaction.

So she hadn't been totally unappreciative. Was she still reeling, like he was? For a second he had a mind to pick her straight back up again, carry her to his bed, and ravish her properly, but one more blast from her blow-torch glare, made him put that thought on hold.

'What?' He made one short inscrutable exclamation.

He might as well get in first here, if Miss Not-so-frosty-after-all was going to turn arctic on him, although now he looked closely, she seemed to be more volcanic than polar. He adjusted his jeans again – erection still barely contained – and flashed her an inscrutable boyish grin.

'You can't pull the 'indignant of Edgerton' stunt on me – you enjoyed that as much as I did, and you know it. You only need to look at the state of your n...'

Her formidable shout stamped on his words.

'Stop it Brando! That's enough!'

Great, he'd got her riled. Miss Buttoned-up-tightly was unravelling. One more nudging push to get his own back for how far she'd pushed him. 'Do you know how sexy you look when you're annoyed? I still think you should go with the nipple shield idea – if we're going to have film crews around regularly that is.' He could practically feel the steam coming off her, and he bit his lip to keep his laughter in check as he watched her flush scarlet, then threw in a placatory after-thought. 'Still, it's up to you, obviously.'

He'd leave it there. In the unlikely event that she turned the tables, and retaliated by talking about erections of another sort, he wouldn't have a leg to stand on. Another twitch at his belt failed to ease the constriction. An avaricious, grasping opportunist she might be, but boy, she was hot!

'Yes, thank you, it *is* up to me!' Her snapped hiss zipped across the hall, and razored him like a sharpened penny.

'And you're sure you don't want me to whisk you to bed as part of this morning's country house experience?' His offer was on the table, and he was beyond ready for action. Knowing he was in for a straight rebuff, but he couldn't resist throwing that in, if only to luxuriate in the scowl she fast bowled him.

He grinned, broadly. 'I'll take that as a no, then, shall I?'

When she didn't bother to reply he watched her collect herself, sniff, shuffle, pull her sweater down again. *Jeez, he loved how the fabric hugged her curves, leaving nothing to the imagination.* He'd definitely have to lay off the boob quips. He'd hate her to stop pulling her sweater down like that.

She raised her head, looked him straight in the eye, and dished out a chilling smile that somehow managed to both dazzle and freeze him at the same time. 'So what about the organising?'

An admirably fast recovery, he noted, coupled with a change of subject. Wise move. The only problem was he had no idea what she was talking about.

'Organising?' He screwed his face up, trying hard not to think about the oral explosion they'd just shared, or the fact that his erection was in immediate danger of going into orbit, and tried instead to concentrate on whatever she was alluding to. He didn't get there.

He cocked her a questioning eyebrow.

'Well from what I saw on TV, or rather, from what Bryony told me, I got the impression that Edgerton was in complete chaos, and that I was going to be able to help sort it out. Organising? Streamlining? System implementation? You know, the stuff I do?'

His spirits sank. *Bryony told me...* Why did that phrase always have an ominous ring? 'I'm afraid Bryony is too damn good at misappropriating the truth as everyone else knows it, in pursuit of her own ends.' He shook his head, apologetically. 'The thing is, the TV crew did mess things up for dramatic effect when they were here before, but putting things to rights again was part of the deal too. Most of the rooms in the house are in perfect order under their dust sheets – admittedly they're full of profoundly depressing antiques, which I'd personally shudder to spend ten minutes with, let alone a lifetime, but that's heritage for you. And as you've probably seen, Mrs McCaul keeps the rest of Edgerton in pretty good shape, with a generously large staff, and mostly there's no-one here to tidy up after anyway. Organising just isn't an issue.'

He watched her smile fade, and an expression of quiet desperation creep across her face.

Crikey.

How could anyone look *that* put out just because they'd been told there wasn't any work to be done? This was not the way to go. He needed to keep her calm, relaxed and amenable, so he could push on with his bed-the-husband-hunter plans ASAP. Jeez, he didn't have all year, he needed to think on his feet!

'I thought we'd leave work for today, if that's okay with you? But now I come to think of it, I'm sure my office would benefit from a spot of streamlining, so we can get onto that tomorrow.' There. He was winging it, but it was sounding good! Bryony wasn't the only one who could play around with the truth. 'As for today, I thought I could show you around a bit, take you to lunch, we could go for a walk around the Estate?'

He paused for her reaction. Somehow he'd expected her to look more enthusiastic.

'I was really hoping to get my teeth into something straight away.'

His vision blurred momentarily, at the fleeting thought of what *he'd* like her to get her teeth into. He racked his brain wildly, trying to think of an implementation task that centred around a king-sized bed, and failed.

'Come on, it's obviously important that we get to know each other, given that's what we're both here for. I'm not going to be staying forever, you know!' He gave a rueful grimace at the thought that by rights he should have been back in London last night, and another at the realisation that he was having to push this audacious gold-digger so hard to make her begin her prospecting.

But after the taste of her he'd just had, he knew he wouldn't be going anywhere without tasting more.

* * *

'Another boy's toy!'

Shea rolled her eyes as the sleek sports car scrunched towards her on the gravel. It wasn't just the car she was reacting to. She was accustomed to wealthy men and their expensive cars, but something in Brando's childish exuberance as he sat behind the wheel made her sigh hard and shake her head in despair.

He threw open the door for her, and she climbed in, aware of him scrutinising her legs, inch by inch, from her dizzy heels to

45

her jean-clad thighs, as she slid into the car.

'Snug fit!' She wriggled down into her seat, and raised her eyebrows as she pulled on her seat belt. She shot him a smile. 'Or would you rather call it cosy?'

Cosy. That was his word. Cosy, in his sitting room last night. *Cosy, how she'd felt in his arms this morning.*

She shuddered at the recollection, and shuddered again at how treacherous it made her feel. The heat of his body as he had gripped her tightly to his chest had been sweet agony. She'd spent a lot of last night reliving the moments when he'd carried her into the house as she'd arrived, longing, in the those wakeful, early hours, for an action replay. Thankfully by morning she'd beaten that misplaced desire back into line again, but the moment he swept her into the air for a second time, she was ashamed to admit she hadn't fought him. She'd simply given in to the dizzy thrill. That was even before *that* kiss.

'Everything okay?' His husky question dragged her back to reality with a shiver that zithered through her, and ended between her legs.

'Just so long as you keep to your side.' She shifted in her seat, kicked her lust into line, and flipped a placatory smile in his direction.

'As if I'd do anything else.' His reply was way more indignant than it should have been, given the small matter of that furnace of a snog.

Her heart was still skittering, still refusing to pump normally, and her insides seemed to have dematerialised. She knew that kiss was wrong.

Wrong. Wrong. Wrong.

And she shouldn't let it happen again. Couldn't let it happen again.

Wouldn't let it happen again.

'Are you shaking?' He looked at her with lazy amusement. 'Don't worry! There's no danger of me diving on top of you given the space restrictions. The worst I might do is put a hand on your knee, and even that would be difficult.'

As she closed the door, the full impact of his scent hit her, and she fought a sudden urge to grab him. Where the heck had that come from, and what's more, how was she going to deal with it? She floundered for something to comment on other then the impracticality of the car.

'A lot of my clients have expensive cars, but I've never accepted a ride in one before.' *Maybe I shouldn't have now.* The engine was roaring like a jet plane, and Brando accelerated with such force, her head was thrown back against the head-rest.

'Sorry about that! I haven't driven this baby for a while.' He turned and flashed her a sheepish grin, raising his voice to be heard over the engine noise. 'The sheer power always takes me by surprise, but it's a great way to blast away the tension.'

At least he was slightly less fanciable when spinning the wheels like an idiot, so long as she kept her eyes away from his hard muscular thighs. And his beautiful, tanned fingers tapping on the steering wheel. And the lump of his Adam's apple in the column of his neck. And... dragging her eyes away, she forced out a reply. 'Obviously. Though the scenery is just a blur when you're doing triple the speed limit.'

'You scared?'

One heart stopping flash of a grin from him she could have done without there.

'Nope.' She wasn't sure if it was his gritty strength or his air of über-cool, but somehow she felt safe. A lot safer than when he'd grabbed her.

'It's Edgerton. The damned place stresses me like nothing else.' His face contorted in a bitter grimace. He dragged his fingers through his hair, rubbed the stubble shadow on his jaw, shook his head distractedly and closed his tanned fingers around the wheel again. 'Give me twenty miles and I'll be better.'

She tried to concentrate on something other than how beautiful he looked.

'Everyone has their own problems. Money and wealth are no guarantee of a happy life. I see that on a daily basis with the people I work for. Anything I can do to help?' She felt she had to ask, even though she doubted she could do anything to help a guy this twitchy.

'You could kiss me again...' His voice was low and he turned his face towards her for a moment. The broad, pushing-it, cheeky grin she anticipated wasn't there. What was left of her stomach plummeted as she met his serious, stone-grey gaze. *Oh lordy.*

'Nice try, but you can forget that!' She tried for a forceful, angry, no-nonsense snap, but it came out shakily. She hoped he hadn't clocked that tremor.

'Always worth asking, I guess.' He came right back with a flashy smile that held for a second, before it fell away. 'It did work – the kiss, I mean. It melted the stress right away – for a while at least.'

Nice to know. Not.

Strange how he'd chosen the word melt, seeing as he'd given her a complete melt down in the process. So typical of men like him. She'd seen it over and over, the way the rich guys kept women on hand to help them de-stress but nothing more. So, Brando was no different. There was no reason why he should be. It was only to be expected, and she wasn't here to judge. But neither was she here to share kisses with him. Alarm bells were clanging loud and clear in her subconscious, but they were only reminding her what she already knew. Women like her didn't mess with guys like Brando.

And she would do well to remember that.

'I'm not some kind of stress-buster.' That came out far more indignantly than she'd meant it to. No need to give him any clue to her thinking. 'What about all your gymnastics? It was you I saw throwing yourself at the trees in the park wasn't it? Doesn't that calm you down?'

She heard him explode into a guffaw of laughter.

'That's not gymnastics, it's free running. Also known as parkour, though if you don't know where Oxford is, you're forgiven for not knowing about parkour.'

She shot him a dirty look in retaliation for that jibe, and for everything else he was doing to her without even knowing, but he carried on regardless.

'It's all about freedom, about running through the environment, reacting to whatever comes, making instinctive moves. It's about breaking the laws of gravity, ultimate fitness, adrenalin, endorphins, and it's best done in cities – there just isn't enough concrete round here to make it work. That's why I end up running at trees.'

'So what you're saying is that it doesn't de-stress you? Not even after all that exercise?'

'It should, but it doesn't always work. Not here.'

She gave a disparaging grunt. Anything that looked so vigorous had to do something, surely.

'You don't sound very impressed.' His swift sideways look demanded an elaboration.

'It's not about being impressed. It just seems an odd thing for a playboy to do.'

'Who says I'm a playboy?' It was his turn to sound indignant now.

'It's blindingly obvious that you're a playboy!' She turned on him, lashing out because he'd shaken her up when he kissed her, but more so because she'd shaken herself up remembering she should have nothing to do with him. Attack was her only way to slap him back into line.

'You're a one hundred percent playboy! Through and through! And what's more, you're totally predictable. You only have to look at your house, your car, even that kiss, for chrissakes. All bog-standard, predictable choices for a playboy.'

She was lying about the kiss of course. The thought of it made her insides whirl, and her head go dizzy. She'd never experienced anything like that in her life before. That kiss had been anything but predictable, which was why she needed to mention it now. She needed to drag it into the open, parade it, hang it out in public, and mark it as worthless. Somehow lumping it, burying it, along with this whole rant helped to rubbish it, helped to show him she was dismissing it. This way he'd know it meant nothing to her, nothing at all… Even though it did.

'Okay, I hold my hands up.' He was sounding conciliatory now, patronising even. 'I've got a big house and a flash car. As for the kiss, whatever you believe, I *don't* go around snogging the face off every woman who crosses my path. And I hold up my hands to wild and bad. Okay, I get my kicks from no-ties sex, yes I get with lots of women who like the same, no I never remember their names, even though they invariably tell me. But I'd hardly claim to be a playboy.'

She took a moment to get her head round the information spill. And another to batter down a ridiculous pang of jealousy for the women who made it to his bed. On the bigger scale, she sensed she was gaining ground here, and she wasn't about to back down when she was about to win the argument.

'Okay. So how long do your relationships last? On average?'

She watched his jaw drop. Saw him pick it up again. Wondered if she'd pushed too far.

'It depends. I'd say, on average, what…' He hesitated. 'My relationships, if you choose to call them that, usually last anything between twenty minutes and five hours, give or take a few seconds. Five hours is usually the tops.'

He flashed her a triumphant smile.

She felt her own jaw drop. She considered if he was winding her up, and decided that he wasn't. What the heck was there to say to that? She struggled to think of an appropriate reply.

'Thank you for answering that, I appreciate your honesty Brando.'

'If you knew me better you'd know the truth is something I value highly Shea, something I demand of myself *and* others.' He cut in harshly.

'I guess that makes you an honest playboy then!'

She was suddenly aware that she needed to move this conversation on quickly. The last thing she wanted was to have him ask her the question in return. If he was demanding truth, she couldn't bear to have to tell him her relationships lasted no time at all, because she didn't have any. She'd backed herself up this blind-alley, and now she needed to get out of it fast.

'Perhaps you need to think about a more sensible car, Brando, then maybe a more sensible lifestyle would follow!' She cringed at how judgemental that sounded. No idea where that had come from, but she could already see steam coming from his ears, so as a diversionary tactic it had worked a treat.

'You sound just like Bryony!' His loud complaint had the vaguest touch of a whine about it.

Good move. Her lips curved into a smile of relief. He wouldn't be going back to relationship questions now. She waited, let her next comment hang in the air a few seconds before she dropped it, because she knew it was going to drive a commitment-phobe like him up the wall.

'Well, let's face it, you're never going to fit a wife and three kids in this car are you Brando?'

Whoops!

She held onto her seat tight as the car left the road, took a trip onto the verge, then jolted back onto the tarmac again.

Result! That had sent him firmly into orbit, as predicted. Game to her!

He shot her a killer of a scowl, which she regretted immediately. Feeling moody made him look like he'd just dropped off the page of a Vogue photo-shoot, which was altogether more hunk than she could cope with right now. And a swift recovery like that only went to emphasise his status as a seasoned player.

'If you promise to keep your life-coaching to yourself, Miss Roll-in-the-hay Summers, I might be persuaded to buy you lunch! How far from playboy does burger and chips sound?'

'Brando, you can't park here, you're on double yellow lines!'

Brando reeled at the speed of her reaction as he pulled up at the kerb in what seemed to him, little more than a village, but what passed in these parts for a town.

She was onto him before he'd even turned the engine off, dammit.

'All part of the fun of being a playboy! I park where I like, and my PA pays the fines later! Let's face it, the absence of tow-trucks for bad parkers is the only upside to life in the sticks.' He sent her an unrepentant smirk, expecting that to be the end of it, but she rapped straight back at him.

'Grow up, Brando! There's a car park the other side of the wall. Stop behaving like a child and go and park there!'

Who the hell went postal over something as minor as double yellows? She was reminding him more and more of Bry here, and not in a good way. But her exasperated cry slapped him into action, and before he knew it he was manoeuvring carefully into the centre of a marked parking bay.

'Control freak comes out of the closet, or what? That good enough for you, Shea-rhymes-with-do-what-I-say?' He hoped his query was mocking enough to hide his inner shock.

Since when had he done what some woman ordered him to? And what's more he'd done so without so much as a question. Hell, he'd offered no resistance whatsoever. He'd just obeyed. Sure, the image he liked to portray was laid-back and cool, but ultimately, beneath the chilled veneer he was *always* the one in control.

'For future reference, I'm the one who gives out the instructions round here. I have a converted warehouse full of employees in London, who all answer to me. They do it because I'm the one who puts my head on the block, I'm the one who takes all the risks. I'm the boss, dammit, I don't take "do as you're told" from anyone, and that includes you!' He tapped the steering wheel, hoping he'd made his point.

'Sorry Brando, but if you behave like a complete jerk, I will tell you.'

There she was again. Straight back, fighting. And she was so sexy when she did. There was definitely something different about this woman and the game she was playing. He just hadn't quite worked out what it was yet. She was fumbling in the footwell for her bag now.

'Are you going to mess around all day there, or are we going for lunch?' Annoyance merged with frustration, leeching through his impatient bark, and he thought he caught a flicker of consternation on her face, but when she turned to him she was smiling a winning, confident smile.

'One minute for lip gloss, then I'm all good!'

'Lip gloss!' He gave a double groan. The first, a small one, for the high-maintenance women he dated, and their preening, make-up laden lives, which he had so far managed to steer admirably clear of, the second, a larger, full-blown, shudder as he thought of the taste of her lips when he'd kissed her.

That kiss.

The thought of it sent an ocean tide roaring through his ears. However she'd tried to dismiss it, he *knew* she'd been kissing him back, kissing him hard, kissing him like a demon.

Damn women, damn their lip gloss!

As he slammed his car door, he was aware of her on the other side of the car's low roof, unfolding, smoothing her jeans, stretching.

'Almost there!' She sent him a half mocking smile with the merest hint of apology.

The sheer anticipation of the moment when she pulled her jumper down tight over her jutting breasts had already sent his blood pounding downwards, and suddenly he knew the reason for his unbearably wound-up state, the reason this morning's free running had offered him no release.

It was her. And the problem was simple. She was racking his desire to levels he was failing to handle.

The more time he spent with her, the more his already heightened libido was rocketing to crazy places. He cursed himself for neglecting the sexual side of his life over the last few months. Not that he'd actually thought about it much. Maybe he was getting old, maybe he was just too busy, but however hot the sex, somewhere along the line, the faceless repetition had ceased to thrill him. Perhaps if he'd given it more priority, he wouldn't be in this state now.

So much for his boasts about being wild and bad.

He couldn't particularly remember a time when he'd had this exact sense of urgency before, but he knew for sure there was only one answer to the immediate problem.

He needed to bed Shea Summers, and he needed to do it fast.

Chapter Four

Perched on high leather-clad chairs at the bar which ran the length of the restaurant, Brando studied Shea as she opened her mouth to take a gigantic bite of burger, noticed how neat and even her teeth were, and pushed aside an overpowering desire to crash his lips over hers.

Jeez. He needed to stop being ridiculous. Okay, her eye teeth might be deliciously pointy. So what? He leaned back on his chair, and idly let his eyes slide down as far as her crossed, denim-clad knees, which were almost touching his own.

He forced himself to look up again. To sound laid-back, he asked 'Want some ketchup? This place is so exclusive, we've got our own bottle! The Beef Box is where London escapees come when they're pretending to be locals, by the way. Rumour has it the fries are individually hand-crafted.'

'I've tasted the love already.' She smiled as she pushed another chip into her mouth, and caught a stray onion with her little finger.

'Good burgers?' He grasped his own mega-stack with both hands.

Not, he hoped, quite what the lady was expecting for her stately lunch out, but all the more fun for wrong-footing her.

She nodded at him in vigorous appreciation. 'Great thanks, couldn't be better! Burgers are my fave, but I haven't had one for ages. This is a brilliant place, have you seen their ice cream flavours? They're stonking!'

Loving the burgers, stonking ice cream flavours?

Perhaps not so great, then, as a means of knocking her off her stride.

It looked like he was back to the plan of getting her into bed happy. He might yet have to pin his hopes on the champagne ice cream.

'So have you had Edgerton Hall long?' Her question, bouncing up off the stainless steel counter, took him by surprise.

Boy, this woman didn't waste time. He wasn't sure he was ready for any conversation, let alone this one. He preferred to cut straight to the sex, which would be no bad thing here either.

'I guess the house has been in the family for generations.' He posted her a vague smile. No harm in fudging the issue, making her work for her information.

'No, I mean you personally.'

Straight in, and going for the jugular.

'I inherited when I was twenty.' He took another bite of burger.

'Which was...?' She eyed him quizzically, as she turned her bun.

'Fifteen years ago.' He watched her suck a slick of ketchup off her middle finger. If that was meant to soften him up, it was working. *Like a truth drug.* 'It wasn't supposed to come to me. My uncle was due to inherit when my grandfather died, but he fell off his yacht. As he had no family, my father would have been next in line, but as he'd died already it passed to me. Quite a surprise.'

And way too much information. Aware that her mouth was already forming the next question he jumped in fast, nodding towards the bulging bags she'd been clutching earlier, after a lightning dive into the local shops.

'So what have you been buying then?'

She eyed him darkly, suddenly guarded. 'Supplies.'

He'd managed to divert her, even if the information she'd given was non-specific.

'Supplies?' He raised one eyebrow, sensing hesitation. Had her cheeks turned pink?

'Okay. Bags of kiddie sweets. Sour worms, cola bottles, Dracula's teeth – ' she grimaced, then spun him a guilty smile. '– fizzy fish, psycho skulls, strawberry laces. Need I go on? I eat them non-stop, okay, and Edgerton's isolated. I've had to do a bulk buy.'

Before he'd done snorting, she'd already fired the next question.

'So what's in *your* bags?'

Tactical error. *Damn.* He'd blown this one. 'Supplies.'

She cocked her head at him in query.

Bulk buy of condoms – how would summer-day-Shea take that one?

'Believe me, you don't want to know.' He flashed her one wicked grin. 'How about we look at the pudding menu?'

* * *

By the time they'd rounded everything off with coffee, it was mid-afternoon when they staggered back to the car. They'd called in the local outfitters, and bought Shea some wellies with matching welly socks, a thick parka coat, and a couple of cashmere cardies. At least she was going to be warm now. Warm and hopefully open to suggestion.

'This is what I mean about the car being impractical,' Shea pointed out ruefully, as he posted the bags through the car door, and piled them on top of her.

Brando tried to look nonplussed.

'This car is perfectly fit for its purpose. It's made for driving, not for shopping, simple as!' He snorted dismissively, though for the first time in his life he could see her point. 'Can't say it's ever been used for shopping before, or that it ever will be again! Shea, what's that round your neck?'

As he slotted the box of wellingtons under her chin, and snatched an unscheduled bird's-eye view down her top, he'd caught sight of something hanging from a gold chain, nestling between her breasts. He watched her hand shoot to clutch whatever it was, saw a crimson flush creep over her cheeks.

'Just...' she faltered.

'Just what?' His idle enquiry was hardened by her guilty tone.

She cleared her throat, and her voice was stronger, more assured now. 'I'm not sure it's any business of yours, but it's something I wear all the time. My grandmother's wedding ring.'

She turned to face him now, with a slow, deliberate grin. 'Brownie's motto – "Be prepared." Never know when I might need it! Waiting for Mr Right and all that!'

Of all the...

He flung her door shut, hurled himself around the car and into the driving seat, and slammed his own door.

Now he'd seen it all!

A husband-hunter who travelled with her own ring! How perverse was that?

He revved the engine until it screamed, did one crazy reverse out of the parking space, then banged the car into first gear, and accelerated away like a madman.

Fifteen miles down the road, the fast driving hadn't done anything to reduce his stress. The engine's violent roar had drowned Shea's early protests, and now she was hunched and silent.

Small, vulnerable, unthreatening.

Which only served to underline how misleading appearances could be.

She was very different from the usual hard-nosed party socialites with whom he rubbed shoulders, and lots more. Overtly brash and shallow they might be, but at least they did what it said on the tin. Hell, they were pussy cats compared to the woman beside him. She may not have their veneers of sophistication, but with her girl-next-door looks combined with her predatory personal agenda she was ten times more dangerous.

What exactly was she hiding beneath that high class organiser exterior of hers?

She was ambitious and calculating enough to propel herself into the unknown in the hope of hooking herself a random billionaire. Her sights were firmly set upon his house and his wealth, but it suddenly hit him she could be looking for a whole lot more. He was used to women whose ambition in life was to party, whose main aim was to drink until the champagne ran dry.

But this woman was looking for Mr Right, and that was a whole other ballgame.

The thought hit him like a bucket of icy water.

Who would go round searching for that from random strangers? All the more justification to take her down before he sent her packing. His knuckles turned white as he gripped the steering wheel. Someone definitely needed to show this uptight, calculating woman there was more to life than happy ever after. It would do her good to have the taste of a one-night stand, to be pleasured to excess – his own speciality, and the passing thought sent him rock hard – then left. And he was happy to oblige, to teach her that lesson.

'You can forget about wedding rings!' He roared the words across at her, but the engine's howl devoured them as soon as he spoke them.

He saw her mouthing at him, shaking her head. She obviously hadn't heard then.

Except the noise of the engine was dying now, and the car was dragging, slowing, dawdling.

'What did you say?'

The engine finally spluttered into silence, and the car rolled to a jerking halt.

He spluttered himself, but his was a rising splutter, not a dying one. 'Great! Now we're out of eff-ing petrol! I hope you like walking!'

She turned to him, her eyes wide.

'Was that in the plan?'

She had to be joking? It wasn't planning which had landed them here. Just him driving like a crazy guy in response to her blasted ring. He kicked himself for forgetting that this car did zero miles to the gallon when thrashed, kicked himself again for being in the goddam countryside in the first place. No petrol stations for miles. No mobile signal.

'Well some of us have obviously been putting in overtime with the planning!' His brow came crashing down and he glowered at her accusingly.

'Excuse me?'

Her tiny query didn't temper his anger. He spoke through gritted teeth, his voice a growl.

'Let's get this clear once and for all! There's no place for wedding rings here! If you're looking for Mr Right, you're hitting on the wrong guy.'

* * *

'Keep up!'

Brando barely looked behind him as he barked the words at her, for what had to be the nineteenth time since they'd set off on their cross-country hike back to Edgerton.

Shea blew heavily, and pushed a damp strand of hair off her forehead, as she stumbled over yet another grassy tussock. He'd set off at top speed before she'd even had a chance to do up her coat. She'd been running after his broad back for four fields now, and her lungs and legs were burning. She slowed to a walk, trying to get her breath back, caught her hands in her coat pockets and pulled it around her now. Thank sugar she was doing this in wellingtons and not high heels. Ahead of her she could see Brando had already reached the next fence, and was leaning on it nonchalantly, scratching his head.

Looking disgustingly attractive.

She kicked herself for that thought. He was one screwed-up

guy. Knotted with tension and with the temper of a two year old. The look on his face when he saw the wedding ring, and she'd tried to cover it with a joke! And what a traitress that made her feel. She didn't do men, and she didn't do attraction. Brando was out of the question on every level.

But he did have some crazy male magnetism thing going on. He played havoc with her pulse rate even when he wasn't kissing her, and when he did – well, best not to go there! As it was she was struggling to keep her hands off him. Thank sherbet he was an arrogant bone-head. If he had been in any way a decent guy, she'd have been in huge trouble, regardless of her abstinence policy.

Too much testosterone for his own good. And hers.

Her stomach flipped as his lazy growl grazed her.

'Some time today would be nice...'

Listen to him! Arrogant and condescending didn't begin to cover it.

He levered himself off the rail, and shot her an unexpected sideways grin, which sent prickles skittering down her spine.

Dizzied by hormones? Guilty as charged.

At least he had waited for her. Without warning he sprang into the air, and landed on the other side of the fence.

'Nice vault! You could almost have been teleporting there!'

She needed to keep her confident, in control act intact, however much she might be falling apart inside. She began to clamber over the fence herself, and as she twisted and swung her leg over the top rail he stretched up, grasped her around the waist, then set her neatly on the ground. Wow!

'Not far from home now. Mrs McCaul's husband, Bob, can pick up the car later. We used to walk this way to the pub in the next village when I first came here. Back in the day, and all that.' A distant expression clouded his face momentarily, but at least his tone had softened. 'Come here, I can see I'm going to have to pull you the rest of the way back!'

Before she could protest, his large hand had slipped around

hers and tightened. Despite his heat, she shivered.

'You're cold!'

Except that shiver had nothing to do with the cold. 'Not too bad, my coat's very...'

One more tug and he'd dragged her towards him. Another and he'd slammed her body up against his. The heady scent of hard, clean man engulfed her, whipping away her ability to think, and her will to protest.

One strong hand gripped her back, one rough finger tilted her chin. His eyes, when she met them, were granite flecked, his voice husky, harsh, taunting.

'This *is* what you're here for, isn't it?'

She opened her mouth to contradict, but before she could speak his lips closed in on hers, sweeping away her words and her breath simultaneously.

Hard and raw.

His stubble stung her chin, he tugged on her hair, jolted her head back further as his tongue plundered her mouth, without remorse.

Hot. Demanding.

Irresistible.

She sank against his hard body, hating herself for allowing this, despising the part of her that wanted it, as the bang of his heart reverberated against her breasts.

More delicious than anything she could remember.

As his hold tightened, his erection ground into her stomach, and turned her legs molten. His tongue tangled deeply with hers now, as she fought against a force field that threatened to turn her upside down and shake her. Then just as she was about to collapse, he pulled away. Sagging, she felt his thumb rasp across her throbbing lower lip, then he grasped her shoulders, and studied her with a derisory scowl. Watched dispassionately as she thrashed to get her breath back.

He waited for her gasps to subside before he spoke.

'We need to go and finish this...'

One gruff, non-negotiable order which set her pulse racing again.

A second to take in the chill in his narrowed eyes, against the fading afternoon sky. The set of his jaw. Then he grabbed her wrist with a lurch, and set off towards the next hill.

* * *

Shea Summers. Professional, reliable, cool, detached, capable.

Not.

Twenty four hours away from home, and she'd already snogged the boss. Twice.

Outrageous. Beyond redemption. If that wasn't totally off the rails, she didn't know what was. She was running now, her hand still in Brando's iron grip, but he wasn't hauling her any more. She was somehow floating effortlessly beside him.

Thank liquorice there was no-one here to judge her, apart from herself. She'd gone downhill fast! Her housemates would've had a field-day if they'd known. In her head they were already crowding around her, each giving their own take on the situation, throwing in their warnings and suggestions. Being supportive. And she cringed to think what her parents might say. So many people, who'd put so much effort into to protecting her these last four years, and the moment she was away from them she'd totally lost it. Something so powerful here, it was even eclipsing her guilt pangs. She should be a lot more ashamed of herself than she was.

'Not too far now...'

He shot her a half grin that made her legs wobble. Amazing that one man, who knew no more about her than that she couldn't do geography and that she liked eating burgers, had unleashed this hormonal rush.

He made her feel alive again. And maybe that sudden rush of vitality was why she was keeping the guilt at bay.

Her feet were flying over the ground, her body burning with

63

a radioactive glow.

'That's good…'

Brando ignored her reply. He was a weird combination. Pent up, hard as nails one minute, then slicing straight into her under-belly with unexpected rushes of concern, or flooring her defences with that disarming grin of his. Throw in jaw-droppingly beautiful, sexy beyond belief and explanation – animal magnetism didn't begin to cover his brand of lust-inducing excitement. She didn't like him, and she didn't respect him. But he was a complete stranger, miles away from the claustrophobic judgement of friends, offering the glorious liberation of anonymity.

We need to go and finish this.

Maybe she *could* see the sense in that.

'Still hanging on in there?'

And then there was that chocolate voice.

Technically, he wasn't her employer, he definitely wasn't her friend, and he claimed his relationships lasted around thirty minutes. In fling terms, men like Brando got what they wanted and got out. End of. What if she did give in to that alien, driving urge in the pit of her stomach?

'Just about…'

She wouldn't be messing anyone around with her own screwed-up situation. Sugar, she'd never even considered she might fancy anyone again – and somehow the fast forward nature of the attraction made it feel less of a betrayal – but a quick fling might help her get on with life. Every step made this crazy idea more perfect.

'Okay?'

As he turned to ask, she took in those broad shoulders under the worn denim of his jean jacket, the sculpted shadows of his cheekbones, the hard sneer of his illegally sensuous mouth.

Ideal material.

And the way she was amped up right now, it wouldn't take five minutes, let alone thirty.

It was a win-win situation. No losers. She'd never have to see him again. No-one would know. And afterwards she'd be free.

A shudder of anticipation juddered through her.

'Okay, yep...' *More okay than you'd ever know.*

Brando swung to look at her, as the shiver arrived at his hand. She bit her lip, felt her hot cheeks flush hotter, and flashed him an extravagant grin.

Shea Summers, professional, reliable, cool, and capable, was planning to be very bad.

Chapter Five

Shea lost her wellies by the front door, shed her coat halfway along the landing, tore off her scarf and tossed it on the sofa as she dashed past, and was standing by her bed when Brando caught hold of her shoulders from behind. She'd left the door to her room open, but hadn't been sure that he'd follow her in. Now he was here, his breath, hot on the back of her neck, making her heart jerk against her ribcage.

'Not so fast!' His growl, as rough as his grasp, sent tingles zipping down her backbone. 'What's the hurry?'

What's the hurry?

If only he knew.

It had to be fast, and it had to be now. A moment's hesitation, and she might lose her nerve. Feeling suddenly too small in her socks, she drew in a shuddering breath, attempted to steady her nerves, pull herself together. She lurched forward as he scored his thumbnail lazily across the base of her neck, and sent an electric shimmer zipping through her. She felt her nipples tauten, as the current zigzagged down her body, and landed smack between her thighs with a zap which reminded her *exactly* why she was here.

'No hurry, none at all.' To her relief, the words came out clear and strong. 'In which case, I might as well get some shoes on.'

She padded across the deep carpet, and slipped into some

high patent courts she found lying by the wardrobe. Four inches taller, and definitely empowered, she strode back, smiling strongly now, to face Brando, who was leaning, arms folded, one shoulder nonchalantly resting against the wall.

'Although sometime today would be appreciated...' He was laughing at her now, his voice low and husky, and below one quizzically raised eyebrow she noticed his eyes were darker, and smudgier.

Charcoal, not granite.

He took a moment to study her as she came to a halt in front of him. Even in her heels, her eyes were only level with the open neck of his shirt, and she saw him swallow deeply. With light hands, he spun her around so he was behind her again, and began gently teasing the clips from her hair, letting them fall, one by one, to the floor. She jumped as his teeth found the base of her neck, nipping, gently, as he shook her hair free.

'That's better...'

One more track of a fingernail across her neck.

One more electrically charged shiver, which set every nerve ending in her body jangling.

Slow.

Suddenly slow was good. Slow was exactly what she wanted. Slow, so she could savour him.

Slow and aching.

With a low moan she spun, tilted her head. She stretched a hand out to steady herself, rested it lightly on his chest. The violent thump of his heart under her palm took her by surprise. Breathing raggedly, eyes barely open, she turned her parted lips towards him.

Expectantly.

Bracing herself for a storm.

But when his mouth came down on hers, it didn't crush, it didn't plunder. Instead it was soft velvet, tangling. Hot molten gold, darkly delicious, sweeping her away, demanding her response. Irresistible compulsion, daring her to respond.

So long, it had been so long.

Four years and more, and it had never been like this then.

His hand was grazing her breast, gently teasing through the cashmere, making her cry out through the kiss. Skilled fingers slipping under her sweater, sliding down the cup of her bra, to stroke and tease the aching bud. One side, then the other whilst her nipples peaked, thrusted, wild for attention. He was playing, tormenting, circling, whilst she writhed, helplessly.

Never like this.

She groaned again, curled against him, rubbing her jeans against the thrusting ridge of his erection, soft denim onto hard denim, bending her knees to grind herself onto him, pushing herself to rub the insane pulse that was throbbing between her folds. Suddenly crazily close to the edge here. Dizzy, spinning, gyrating, banging against him now, she parted her legs, opened her mouth wide, and screamed deep into his kiss as her whole body erupted in a spectacular, thundering, jolting explosion of pure pleasure.

* * *

Brando wasn't certain, but he had an idea that might have been the sexiest move he'd ever seen. And he hadn't led a sheltered life.

She was leaning against him now, panting, exhausted, clinging onto his shirt to hold herself up.

Jeez.

And she was still fully clothed.

In one sweeping movement, he scooped her up, deposited her on the bed to recover.

He tried not to think of his own need, bursting as it was. Given what she'd inadvertently revealed to him, that was going to have to wait.

That was the sexiest move he'd seen, yes, but also the most innocent, uncalculated, and guileless. He was still fully clothed, dammit. That had to be the biggest accidental orgasm of the century. Unless she was entirely calculating, and faking, which somehow he doubted. Not even the most cynical of schemers would have dreamed that one up.

'Crikey, awwww, no! That shouldn't have happened! I'm sorry Brando...'

You only had to listen to her to know.

He shook his head, raked a hand through his hair. He watched her lying with her cheeks still flushed, chestnut curls tangled across the quilt, her perfect rosy lips, swollen. Yep, and there was that blasted chain with a ring on, pulled tightly across her throat, disappearing behind her hair.

'Brando?'

Her wide violet eyes, fixed on him, a sudden shiver making her all the more childlike.

How the hell had he got her so wrong?

And how the hell was he going to walk out of this one now?

'Sorry Shea, I need to go...' Even as he muttered the words he was backing out of the room.

Sure, he was wild, and yes, he liked wicked, but even he drew the line at being bad and wicked with nice girls like her. That was simply out of order. Not on.

Bad and wicked were for women who could handle bad and wicked.

And this woman wasn't one of them. He'd get the hell out of here, as soon as.

Dammit, he was loath to walk away.

But it had to be done.

* * *

'Phew!'

Shea put the phone down, some time later, and let out one huge sigh of relief. She'd talked to her mum about everything from her dad's lumbago to whether Jilly from next door was too old to carry off a fringe, without giving anything away about earlier this afternoon.

She'd phoned home early, from Mrs McCaul's office downstairs, hoping to stay clear of Brando until she'd decided what to do.

The blinds on the office windows were up, and as she turned out the lights and prepared to leave, she glimpsed a view across a courtyard. In the wash of the floodlights, she could make out a single storey building, perhaps an orangerie, its dark gable silhouetted against the sky. It was difficult to be sure in the darkness, but she thought she caught a movement. Someone on the roof.

Then the figure plunged from the parapet, fell through the air, hit the ground, rolled, leapt up and ran off.

Liquorice sticks! What should she do now? As she chewed her nail, trying to decide, the figure reappeared on the roof, then plummeted to the ground, rolled, and ran off.

She waited. Watched it happen again. And again. And again.

Then the figure paused on the roof, raised their arm, raked their hand through their hair – and the penny dropped.

Brando. It had to be Brando.

Her stomach went into freefall and stopped somewhere around her knees. She shuddered. It was the same kind of shudder that had rattled up and down her spine non-stop since this afternoon in the bedroom. She'd promised herself not to think about that mind-blowing release, or the way it had left her longing for more, with a longing so strong that it put all traces of guilt into the shadows. One thought of how it felt to rub against that rock-hard denim. The telltale fluttering playing between her legs escalated to a throbbing ache.

It had to be crazy to feel this level of physical desire for a man she didn't even like. But worse was the way her body was so out of control, whenever he was there. It was completely illogical. And illogical was something she didn't do. Ever.

Shea was hooked on logic. A logical approach put her in control of situations and being in control made her feel safe.

When everything else in life failed and control was all you had left, that's what you hung on to. She liked to function in a world where everything had a place and everything had an explanation.

So why the hell did she have the uncontrollable hots for Brando?

Okay. She was away from the pressures of everyday life, away from the scrutiny of family and friends. Add in she'd had no sex for five years.

The sex-starved holiday effect?

Obvious when you thought about it. She gave a low groan.

Perhaps if she'd got away earlier, she might have got a perspective on her life sooner, realised that moving on was the only way forward. It was physical not emotional and that made it easier to handle. One-off no-strings sex, with an irresistible guy? Her chest fizzed at the thought of the freedom that would hand her.

And Brando was made for the job. Guaranteed to walk away the minute it was over. Whether she liked him or not, they didn't come any better than that. And up until an hour ago he had made it perfectly clear what was on offer – all the signals had been there, practically whacking her in the face.

Out of the window, she could still see his silhouette as he hurled himself off the roof, again and again, as if he was stuck in a repeating loop. One guy, pushing it to the limit. There was something of her own obsession she could recognise in him.

Ker-ching! And suddenly, it couldn't be clearer! Brando had the power to set her free, and it was up to her to take her chance! This had to be *the* perfect opportunity. She'd be mad to pass it by. There was the small matter of his cold feet to overcome, but she'd just have to work on that.

If he ever stopped jumping off the roof that was.

She simply needed to screw up her courage, go to him, and take what she needed.

* * *

Much later, standing in the flickering firelight in her room, her resolve hadn't faltered.

It was a while since Brando had come thumping along the landing. The thud of his door closing as he went into his room had set her own heart banging, and it hadn't stopped since then. She had lost just enough clothing to ensure that he would come in from the cold, kept enough on to feel dressed herself. Brushed her teeth, her hair. Put on lip gloss, shoes.

Only one thing left to do now.

She ran her fingers lightly along the chain around her neck, closing them around the wedding ring that hung from it.

For a moment she hesitated, holding the ring, still warm, on her open palm.

She took one deep, juddering breath, to remind herself that what she was about to do had nothing to do with caring.

Then with quick, shaky hands, she undid the clasp, slipped the ring and the chain onto the table, and headed towards the door.

* * *

'Brando?'

It was Shea, and she hadn't waited for his reply. She'd simply pushed the door open, and waltzed on in. Marched through the sitting room, the bedroom, and straight into the office, where he was lounging on a swivel chair, in front of his desk.

'Not working are you?' Shea peered at his computer screen. 'No, I didn't think you would be.'

Brando wondered, in passing, if having an orgasm with someone, fully clothed, somehow bestowed un-negotiated rights of entry on that person. Free passage, or something. Then, as he felt eight pints of blood make a direct rush for his groin, he wished he hadn't thought of it at all.

He shouldn't even have been here now for her to crash in on. He should have been long gone. He was Brando Marshall after all, famous for his lightning fast responses to changing situations. He'd planned to make an immediate get away, by helicopter, car, train, bus. On foot if necessary. Head back to London. In short, he'd been ready to do anything it took to get him away from the hideous temptation of rhymes-with-day Summers.

Except he hadn't. The Brando Marshall fast response instinct had completely failed. The best he'd managed was an hour of throwing himself off the roof of the Orangery.

And he was still here. And now, so was she.

Staring at his computer screen, over his shoulder.

And what the hell was she wearing? Or rather, not wearing?

A whole lot less than she'd been wearing this afternoon, that was for sure.

'Nice shorts! They're great when they're so short they only leave half a bottom to the imagination, aren't they?' He was lying of course. Ideally he wouldn't want *anything* to be left to the imagination, but at the same time, if he was trying to resist her, tiny shorts spelled disaster.

She didn't make a direct reply, but the dimples in her cheeks told him she knew he'd love them.

He definitely wasn't going to play into her hands and mention the fact that her legs were bare and her heels were as towering as something else he could think of. Nor was he going to raise their usual teasing subject of underwear. It would be obvious to a blind man that she wasn't wearing any. No knickers. No bra. He shifted on his desk chair, trying discretely to rearrange his jeans to accommodate the erection of the decade. If things continued in this vein his he'd soon be passing out due to lack of blood on the brain.

'Did you enjoy your dinner?' He decided to try meaningless conversation. Given that she'd come in uninvited, he doubted if she'd leave, even if he asked her. It crossed his mind that this was another instance of him playing into her hands, doing exactly what he wanted him to.

'You might be here to discuss dinner Brando, but I'm not.'

Short, snippy. Told him straight, pulled him up.

'So, what would you like to talk about?' A dangerous, open-ended question. He realised too late he should have put some conditions on that. Forty-eight hours out of London, and he was already losing his edge.

'I came to ask why Playboy-of-the-Year ran out on me back there.' She was leaning in towards him now, dangerously close. Smelling like heaven.

His eyebrows shot skywards. He hadn't expected her to be so direct. So brave. *So sexy.* He thought for a minute, carefully considered her accusing defiance before he answered.

'I play around, you don't. Let's say I thought better of it.' How else to tell her she wasn't the hard case he'd thought she was?

'We're both adults Brando. We can do as we please. I'm not asking for a lot of your time...'

'Yeah, sure. Give me one good reason why you'd want to?'

'Maybe because I need one-off, no-strings sex to move on from something else, and as I read it, you're ready, willing and able. But best of all you're detached enough to do the job, with no repercussions.'

Detached enough to do the job? He wasn't sure if that was flattering or not. So some guy had messed her around, and she needed a revenge lay. That made sense. His brow furrowed, as an unexpected surge of anger swept through him. Why the hell was he feeling furious because some guy had hurt her? It wasn't as if she needed his protection. And it wasn't only anger. A pang of raw jealousy spiked deep in his chest at the thought of her sleeping with someone else.

He smacked himself on the head, hard. Told himself not to be ridiculous. He hardly knew the woman. He *never* got involved enough to feel protective or jealous, that was the whole point. All those years ago, he'd vowed he'd never trust again, or be hurt again. Zero involvement was his strategy for survival. This was beyond crazy.

His cheek twitched as he scraped his fingers through his hair. He pulled himself back to the most immediate problems.

Problem one; how to get rid of this barely-dressed siren, who had now perched her delectable ass on his desk. Whose endless, curvy, sexy leg grazed his elbow as she crossed it.

Problem two; not entirely unrelated to problem one, how to deal with his screaming libido.

It crossed his mind that there was one, glaringly obvious solution, which would solve both problems at a stroke, but he couldn't help feeling that was a solution which, however pleasurable, would bring a lot more problems in its wake.

Well, she'd given him the reason he'd asked for, but he definitely wouldn't be obliging.

'Nah! Can't do it, won't do it. Sorry. It's wrong.'

'I had you down as a risk taker Brando. But if you daren't?'

'It's not that I daren't.'

'Or if you don't want to?'

'It's not that I don't want to.'

'You don't even have to join in.'

What the hell did she mean by that?

As she slipped off the desk and stepped out across the room on her high heels he wondered what had happened to the faltering girl who fell into an orgasm this afternoon. Mesmerised, he span his chair round to watch her. Leaning back a lot more lazily than he felt and ignoring the forging bulge beneath his zip, he tilted his head to one side, raising an eyebrow.

As she turned and moved towards him with a slow determination, her high breasts pushed tight against the thin fabric of her next-to-nothing camisole, and he shuddered as the uninterrupted view of her hard nipples whacked his erection up a notch. Her parted lips trembled slightly, her eyes blurred as they fixed on his groin. Then in one swift silky movement she had straddled him, banging her thigh on the tip of his bursting erection as she landed. He groaned in hot excruciating pleasure. Her hair brushed his neck as she bent, pressing her lips to his ear.

'Stay completely still Brando. I take full responsibility for using you – that way it can't be wrong.' The huskiness of her whisper sent a volley of anticipatory darts shooting down his spine.

The responsible side of his brain told him to stand up, take control, toss her aside, insist that she leave. But the wicked side told him to lie back and let Shea-rhymes-with-do-as-I-say do her worst. Then she shifted. Another exquisite bullseye nudge of her pelvic bone, another intense corkscrew of pleasure, and the full-blown scent of an aroused woman smacked him in the face.

'And what if...' He opened his mouth, attempting a token protest, but her finger was already on his lips, silencing him.

'No more talking! This isn't going to take long, I promise.'

She moved her pelvis backwards, and he reached out a hand to caress one delicious nipple, but she snatched it away in mid air.

'No touching, not yet!'

As she stretched out towards the zip of his jeans, rubbing the heel of her hand across the bursting denim, he heard himself groan again. An expression of deep concentration spread across her face as she parted the denim with her fingers, making jagged tugs at his zip until it was down. He heard her gasp gently as her hand landed on him, explored the length of his shaft through the cotton of his boxers, then she stretched to stand. In one easy movement, she had dragged back his pants, and released him to stand to glorious attention.

'Oh boy...'

He could smell the scent of his own musk rising as he heard her murmured exclamation, saw her bite the corner of her lip, push a cascade of hair off her face.

'Do you have... a condom?' Her whispered query was barely audible. 'Please?'

'In the pocket.' He mumbled, motioned to the jean jacket hanging on the next chair, swallowing hard, his eyes locked onto her breasts as she stretched to retrieve the packet. He saw her fingers tremble as she fumbled to open it, then she flicked him a foil pack without meeting his eyes. Within two seconds, he'd ripped it with his teeth, ready to go.

And how...

'Stay still, shut up, and leave this to me.' One last breathy command.

Unusual approach. That thought, desperately taking his mind off the fact he was already way beyond ready to explode.

Zero foreplay, and he was more wired than he'd ever felt.

Jeez, he didn't give a flying fish how it happened so long as he had her.

Holding on...

She was over him now, the cotton of her shorts catching him as she pulled them aside and eased herself onto him. Gently, slowly. Hot and sweet, slick and tight, but oh, so ready. He forced himself to think of anything other than the exquisite tornado of heat which burned deep into his core. Fixed his eyes on her face as she took every last inch of him. Watched her features blur. She grasped his shoulders now, pushing herself away, burying her nails in his muscles, as she moved. Grinding, pumping, gyrating, pleasuring herself on his length. She was throwing her breasts high, arching as she rode him mercilessly, panting, crying out.

He was waiting, waiting, waiting, dying...

Then she flung back her head, and he knew he could give in. Let go. One thrust, and the first convulsion of her body propelled him to the most wringing, wrenching, ecstatic orgasm of his life.

He heard her let out a long moan, moving with the rise and fall of her sea. He felt her disintegrate around him, fall onto his chest and lie, motionless.

Then there was only the sound of their rough breathing and his own banging heart.

* * *

That was it then.

The best climax ever, they still had their clothes on, and he hadn't touched her, let alone kissed her. Some kind of victory for Miss Uptight here.

She was disentangling herself, climbing off him now. Wide eyes, and a smile that was only for herself.

'Thanks for that. I told you it wouldn't take long. Hope it wasn't too wrong.'

And I remember telling you you'd be begging for it. I just didn't think it would be so soon.

Standing up, smoothing her crumpled camisole, checking her watch. Then she shot him one wicked, sideways grin. 'Five minutes. Congratulations Brando! You have a new relationship record.'

Brando studied her through narrowed eyes, as he struggled to zip himself back in.

'This isn't a relationship, Shea.'

Best to keep her straight on that. One hell of a climax, maybe, and his body was telling him in no uncertain terms that it wasn't the end of it. He was fighting to do his jeans up even now, dammit. But a relationship, it was not.

'Too right it's not, Brando!'

Both on the same page there then. That was good. But that couldn't be the end of it.

Not yet.

'I seem to remember mentioning five hours.' He leaned back on the desk, rubbed the side of his thumb pensively across the stubble on his chin. 'So you've used me, and now it's my turn to use you – for whatever remains of those five hours that is!'

Halfway to the door already, that thought jolted her to a halt.

He watched her hesitate. Scanned her opaque expression for some clue as to what she was thinking. Found himself holding his breath.

This was crazy.

When did he ever hold his breath?

Quite simple. He didn't. Ever. Not for anything or anyone.
But then when had he ever wanted something, needed something,
   this much?

Chapter Six

'HI, I'm Shea, and I'm here to help.'

She made her cheery greeting as brusque, yet impersonal, as she could as she strode into Brando's office next morning. She wasn't sure if it was due to embarrassment, excitement or shame, but she felt like she was going to die of something, and boy, was she desperate to hide it. Mrs McCaul had relayed Brando's order for her to be here at nine sharp when she'd delivered the breakfast Shea had been too distracted to touch. Standing in *that* office now, less than twelve hours after *that* event, taking refuge in professional patter seemed the only way to survive.

'Here to help? I'm pleased to hear it!' Brando turned briefly from the desk where he was working, shot her an impassive glance, then carried on flicking through documents on his laptop screen.

Sitting in *that* chair.

Shea swallowed hard, pulled herself up to stand ram-rod straight. Her sharp office outfit was offering none of its usual armour. At least he was acting like it was business as usual, though to judge from the dark shadows under his eyes, it looked as if he'd had as bad a night as she'd had. She'd noticed as she'd passed through his bedroom that his bed hadn't been slept in.

'What would you..?' She began then broke off, not wanting any offer to be misconstrued.

If he noticed her hesitation, he didn't react.

'Help yourself to the cupboards over there – re-organise, stream-line, whatever it is you do. Buy any fixtures, fittings, filing systems, furniture you need, unlimited budget. Do your worst!' His instruction was brusque, and he waved his hand towards the tall doors in the alcove by the fireplace, without bothering to look up.

So much for her worries about him flirting. He barely seemed aware she was even there. A pang of disappointment made her stomach drop.

So that was it then?

She moved across to the cupboard knowing she should feel relieved, but somehow she didn't. The cupboard doors creaked open to reveal shelves of mayhem that would usually have made her heart race with anticipation, but this morning they left her strangely unmoved. She grabbed a pad, ready to make an assessment of the contents, and mentally kicked herself for wanting anything to be different.

Last night, she'd been certain Brando was going to follow her back to her room, and she'd been so ready to give him a hard time. But he hadn't come, and sitting alone in the firelight her body had ached for him, ached for more of the incredible pleasure he'd given her twice already.

She picked up a pen to start her list, hardly believing this was happening to her.

One-off sex to set her free? She shouldn't want any more. That was how it was supposed to be, wasn't it? One great idea that had turned right round and bitten her on the bum, because all the one-off, no-repeats sex seemed to have done was to awaken some mighty dragon of lust and desire in her, and right now the dragon was roaring for more.

But she was determined she wouldn't give in it.

She put down her pad and pen, and instead grabbed a box and transferred it to the table. Then she collected another.

'Having fun?'

Her heart triple-flipped at Brando's lazy enquiry, and she stamped it back into place before she replied. 'You bet!'

'I hope sorting Edgerton's cupboards is living up to expectations. I can't think why you'd want to, but I promised you could, so here you are.' The hard stare he fired across the room at her was at odds with his mocking tone. 'I always do what I say I'm going to, you need to remember that!'

Whatever that meant. Not that she was about to waste time working out his indecipherable asides.

'I need to stay busy.' *Damn.* She said that with the light smile as planned, but it sounded way more desperate than she'd intended.

She saw him roll his eyes.

'I know you like to be in control and for everything to be in order, but even so it's an unusual choice of profession.'

She shrugged, started to gabble nervously. 'I enjoy the job, every day is different. After uni I was hoping to work with textiles, but my aunt decided I had the skills to be an exclusive personal organiser, gave me a job with her company, and I run the Manchester branch now.' At least she'd managed to stop the flow before letting slip that she'd been tidying obsessively to cope with a life that had collapsed when her aunt had seen her potential, swept in and set her to work. She nodded towards the growing pile on the table. 'So what am I doing with this lot? Clients usually want to sort through things. Do you?'

'Hell, no! Bring order to the chaos, that'll do me.'

'Nice and simple. I'll get some co-ordinating boxes and files. Make it look good.' She sniffed, not knowing why she was saying anything more. Rambling was such a bad idea. 'Downsizing jobs are the hardest ones I do, trying to help people get rid of things they think hold the key to their memories.'

She caught his grimace, as she said that, sensing she'd inadvertently strayed onto a sensitive area. When she'd first arrived she'd revelled in uncovering his weaknesses, but today if she'd hit a nerve she was beyond ready to back off.

'Don't worry, I tell my clients it isn't the house that's important, it's the people in it. I'm sure you could be very happy here if you had things around that were a bit less historic, and a bit more like you. Perhaps all the TV presenter was trying to do was to make this lovely house a happier place?'

She watched a shadow cross his face. Then he got up, sauntered across the room, leant a shoulder against the wall nearby, and folded his arms. Before she could stop herself, her gaze had honed right in on his groin. Sugar. Ogling or what? Her knees sagged as she focused on the length of him pushing against the taut denim. Swallowing hard, she dragged her eyes up to his face.

'Well, Do-as-I-say-Shea, if you've finished analysing my needs, perhaps it's time we talked about you.' His sideways smile, at once languid yet unnervingly hard, sent a trickle of dread down her spine that turned into a waterfall. 'After all, you're the one who seems to have something to get over, ghosts to lay and all that.'

She flinched at the word 'ghosts'. She knew she'd needled him, and now it was his turn to needle her back. With any luck, if he'd noticed, he'd assume she was flinching at the word 'lay.'

'Whatever...' she replied only because she knew he would expect it, but didn't look at him.

'You do know the way you did it last night didn't count? The sex, I mean.' His casual, yet measured remark hurtled out of the blue. Hit her broadside.

Business as usual, then he wallops her with something like that?

'What?' This time she stared straight at him, eyes uncontrollably wide.

'If you're trying to put the past behind you, last night isn't going to do anything for you.' He raked his fingers through his hair, then rubbed his thumb slowly on his cheekbone.

The same thumb he'd teased across her breast yesterday. The same one that took the colour out of her skin when it pushed into her thigh last night. Two stomach-squelching thoughts there.

'I don't know what you're talking about.' She had to protest.

83

Except she did know. She knew very well. Taking him was a whole world away from letting him take her.

He was looking at her now, in that same, direct, horribly unnerving way he had when he asked if she was wearing underwear, as if his granite eyes could bore straight through her clothes. Except now they drilled straight through to her soul.

Stripped her way beyond bare.

She fought to get a grip of her somersaulting stomach, and the sudden fizzing desire that was pulsing through her, and prayed that he couldn't see the half of it.

'You know exactly what I'm talking about. The revenge sex. It's only going to count when someone does it to you.' He leaned towards her, his eyes suddenly smoky, his gravelly voice soft. 'I'm not going to push it, but you only have to ask...'

As if.

Then he ran *that* thumb down her cheek in a rough caress that sent anticipation galloping through her body.

He pulled away.

'I'll leave you to your work then!'

Her legs were melting, she was fighting to keep her balance, but before she'd collected herself enough to tell him she'd never be asking him for anything of the kind, he'd already turned and left the room.

* * *

'You still here? I bought you some sweets by the way.'

He thumped a bulging bag down on the desk. Not that she needed them.

Since he'd left Shea this morning Brando had done three hours of vigorous running, then wasted a lot of time in town. He had no idea how anyone could have the patience to spend that much time ferreting in a cupboard, even if it was a huge one.

'I'm almost done here, until the new files and boxes arrive, that is. And thanks for the sweets by the way. I've gone through loads today. I'm already out of sour worms. As for the cupboard, it feels a bit strange just putting everything back without sorting it. You do know the stuff in here is from ages ago don't you?' She stood back, and, avoiding his eyes meticulously, surveyed the impeccably neat shelves instead, a satisfied smile playing around her lips.

He stood behind her. Allowed himself one look at the way her pencil skirt skimmed the curves of her bottom. As his blood rushed to one very pre-determined destination, he knew he'd been right to leave her alone, get the hell out of here this morning. There was no way, after last night, he could have watched her for a whole day without devouring her.

'To be honest I don't know what's in there, and I don't really give a damn!' He spoke without thinking, saw her face fall as the words came out, and immediately started backtracking. 'I mean it's all old stuff, probably mostly forgotten, and it's great that it's all in order now. Brilliant in fact. Did you come across anything exciting?'

Serious grovelling.

When the hell did he do serious grovelling? Why the hell did he feel the need to do it now?

'Professionally, I wouldn't usually comment, but as you've mentioned it...'

The only answer he'd expected to hear was 'no.' She was hesitating now, obviously waiting for his permission to go on.

'Well?'

'There's a load of band stuff in there.'

Jeez. What the...? Everything to do with the band was supposed to be locked away in the ballroom. *Damnation.* He'd never have let her in the cupboard if he'd known.

'A band called Take a Bullet? I didn't know you were in a band.' She held up a creased flyer, and raised a quizzical eyebrow.

He took a moment to reel, to get his excuses together. He needed to work out how to move the conversation on and take the thundering kick in the gut of seeing Nick, alive, a belligerent grin on his face, hand slung casually over his own shoulder.

'The band was a long time ago.' He shrugged, diffidently. 'Why *would* you know about the band, when the sum total of what you know about me is that my name is Brando, and my least favourite place is Edgerton Hall!'

Except you know how it feels to sit on me and come.

He forced that thought as far out of his head as he could, in the interests of keeping the maximum brain power to steer her away from the subject of the band, but he could see she was going to press on.

'I was probably only about nine at the time, but you guys must have been big, judging by the awards, and I love the album covers, I bet there's a load of footage on YouTube...'

His best bet was to appear open, give her something more to get her teeth into.

'Take a Bullet are ancient history. YouTube is the only place you'll find them now. Yes, we made a load of money, and I took mine and moved on to business. I still do production occasionally, sometimes promotion or festivals, but these days I deal in risk investment. Big risk means big money. Risk is where I get my buzz, and the billions that come along with it are simply a happy side effect.'

Here's hoping that the information dump would distract her.

'Who'd have thought...' She looked up pensively. 'Talking of buzz, do you have any more storage that needs assessing?'

Result. A natural subject change. Heat off. Easy as. And who, except this girl would get from business-buzz to storage in one crazy leap?

But he was hitting a dead end on this one too.

'Sad to say, you just blitzed my only personal cupboard. The rest are all Mrs McCaul's responsibility, so I'll have to talk to her on that.'

'Okay, thanks – it's just I'm bad at sitting round with nothing to do.' She shot him a pleading smile, which tugged his brain onto more pressing matters.

'I can call on you this evening for the four hours fifty five you owe me. That'll give you something to do!'

Float the idea, see where it goes.

If her thunderous eyebrows were anything to go by...

'I'd thought I'd made it perfectly clear earlier, I'm not going to have sex with you again!'

Her shrill protest was saying one thing but her nipples, pushing taut against the cotton of her regulation office shirt told a very different story. Funny how he couldn't remember her saying anything of the sort.

And when she looked as fiery as she did now, it took every inch of his willpower not to carry her off to bed there and then.

'Who said anything about having sex?'

He flashed her a wicked grin, and watched her cheeks turn scarlet. 'I was going to suggest taking you out for dinner, but if you've got a better idea...'

'No, dinner will be fine.' She jumped in with her reply. 'Thank you, dinner sounds good.'

The woman's ability to make lightning recoveries was awesome.

'We'll go somewhere warm. And I promise to park impeccably.' He was going all out to sound practical and reassuring. 'You can wear your little black dress.'

Your lace stockings.

But all he could think of was taking them off.

* * *

'I brought the most practical car I could find – hope it passes the Shea-test.'

'The leather seats smell nice.' Shea smiled as she ran her hand over the smooth red and white upholstery. 'And I like Minis.'

'Good size parcel shelf, handles well on corners, low fuel

consumption, I thought you'd approve. Though I have to 'fess up, it isn't mine – I've borrowed it from Mrs McCaul.'

Something should've told her a car this sensible couldn't be Brando's.

'Who'd have thought Mrs McCaul would have chosen anything this racy?' She raised her eyebrows in double surprise, first at the thought of a racy Mrs McCaul, then at the speed with which he took the next corner. 'Though a sensible car doesn't always mean a sensible driver.'

He didn't react to that jibe.

'She didn't exactly choose it. She'd always wanted a Mini, and I got it as a surprise sixtieth present for her, last year. Somehow I couldn't bring myself to buy the shopping version. It was just too boring.' Brando sounded suddenly worried. ' Do you think she'd have preferred something less stripy?'

His obvious concern made her smile, want to reassure him. 'I'm sure she loves it. The chrome and the racing logos probably make her feel young.'

'It's their wedding anniversary next weekend, and they're going to London to see Mamma Mia. I always like to make sure they get up to London for a show for their anniversary.'

He almost sounded like he was talking about his parents. So much for Brando treating his staff badly, she'd obviously misread that situation completely.

'Talking about mothers, your mum rang whilst you were in the shower. I assured her you hadn't come to any harm since she phoned this morning, and told her she didn't need to ring again until tomorrow.'

'Brando!'

'What?' He sounded unrepentant. 'She needs to give you more space; you're not a child, she needs to back off and cut the cord!'

'You didn't tell her that?'

He hesitated, ominously. 'Perhaps not in those exact words...'

Which pretty much meant he had. *Damn.*

'You don't understand, if you knew the full picture, you'd know she's only like that because...' Because of all the things she couldn't tell him, and almost had. *Damn again.* Near miss. 'Because she's concerned. And she cares.'

He gave a loud grunt of disapproval, as he flung the car into the car park with a handbrake turn, then came to a screeching halt. She was about to lodge a protest, but stopped as she caught a side view of the deep dimples in his cheeks, illuminated in the yellow light from the pub, and her heart flipped into freefall and took her words clean away.

He grinned across at her triumphantly. 'I think you'll find I'm parked in my marked bay!'

I think you might find you've just run over my heart.

Hands, resting oh-so-casually on the steering wheel.

Strong wrists, beautiful in the half light.

An OMG moment if ever there was one, for all the wrong reasons. When had she ever gone weak looking at someone's wrists? It had to show she was in big trouble.

She needed to slay her lust-dragon, and fast.

* * *

'I can only apologise for the decor.' Brando screwed up his face in distaste, as he leaned back on his chair between courses, and surveyed the surroundings. 'Rustic beams are yet another highly over-rated rural commodity that I hate.'

Shea looked around at the polished stone floor and the slender chairs. As far as she could assess, the timbered building had been stripped back then furnished to give a contemporary, spare yet luxurious feel, which she liked very much. As she was beginning to discover, sometimes Brando was very hard to please.

'So, it's good we're here for the food, not the decor. And the service couldn't be better.'

The tables were large enough for her to keep her distance,

which was the best thing of all, because right now the last thing she needed was for Brando to be too close. If he was drop-dead gorgeous in his everyday denims, the casual jacket and chinos he was wearing this evening had cranked that up to off the scale irresistible. Just enough stubble to... She yanked her imagination to a halt, before she got onto the endless options of where on her body she'd like him to rub it. Whatever the temptation, resist was just what she had to do. She'd had her one-off, and once had to be enough. More was way off limits.

'Anyway, now you've met my mum on the phone, and told me exactly where you think our problems lie, how about your family? I expect they're perfect.'

She knew, even as the words came out, that she could be moving onto dangerous ground. She'd been searching for a subject to take her mind off how much she was lusting after him, wanting to hit out, just a little bit, in retaliation for the way he made her feel so out of control. The way his lip curled into the bitterest of smiles made her wish she could take it back.

'We don't all have sweet, indulgent mothers, and doting, nuclear families. For most people, life just isn't that hunkydory, whatever you think.' The words he'd flung hit the table and splintered up at her.

'I know that, I'm sorry, I shouldn't have mentioned it. And as you pointed out, families can be suffocating, especially when your mum phones three times a day or more.'

She spoke quickly, tried a brief smile. Played the happy family card. She didn't want to give him any cause to guess her background was less than idyllic.

'Three calls or more? That's rough.' He rubbed a thumb over the stubble on his chin. 'I can't remember when I last spoke to my mother. We don't have anything to say.'

Oh my. She'd dragged them into this, now she needed to get them out.

'That's rough too. Just in a different way.' She wasn't pushing for more, but she could tell by the set of his chin that he wasn't done.

'My father left, then died, my mother remarried. I fought with my step-father, was sent away to boarding school and farmed out to friends in the holidays. End of story.'

Or beginning of story, depending where you were sitting. He'd brushed it off, brazened it out. If it hadn't been for a slight twitch in his left cheek and his desolate stare, she'd have believed him.

'What about your sister?' She'd asked before she remembered not to, but suddenly it didn't seem to matter because he was answering without hesitation.

'She was younger when my parents split up. My mother remarried quite quickly, but Bryony never had the problems I did with our stepfather. She pretty much had her own nuclear family, along with a couple of younger half-sisters. She landed in the happy camp.'

'Awwww, Brando.'

'That's the thing. It isn't really 'awww Brando' at all. Boarding school was the best thing that could have happened to me. I was thirteen, a stroppy adolescent, it had been hell at home, and school was great. I made amazing friends, we had the band, I made a load of money, then I got Edgerton. The independence and self-reliance I learned are what you need in life to succeed. Everything I've done, I've done on my own.'

Looking across the table at him now, she wasn't sure if she was looking at a hard-nosed businessman, or that stroppy thirteen year old. She knew hard times made strong men, but what about a life without love? She had a sudden urge to fling her arms around that vulnerable boy. Hug him better. If the table had been smaller, she'd have reached out and put her hand over his. As it was all she sent him was a sympathetic shrug. 'You've done brilliantly, but it still makes me think awwwww a little bit.'

His one raised eyebrow suggested he thought she'd lost her marbles.

'What's not to like?' He snorted his dismissive snort. 'All that's

91

missing are the phone calls.'

The phone calls, and maybe a little bit more.

So she'd been wrong to mark him down as an overgrown spoilt kid, but at least this went some way to explaining his issues. Issues which, she needed to remember, were nothing to do with her. She was here for house organising. Full stop.

She pulled out her brightest, most professional smile, and searched wildly for something trivial to say.

'What's your favourite pudding then?'

* * *

Brando raised an eyebrow in the darkness as he threw the car round the penultimate bend, and realised he was smiling. On the journey back, he'd hardly got a word in edgeways, and she was showing no sign of letting up.

'Choosing puddings has to be one of life's most difficult jobs. Next time I'd definitely have the jam roly-poly. Or it might have to be the sticky toffee pudding. Even now I can't decide, and it's not even happening!'

'So there's going to be a next time?'

That was a showstopper if ever there was one. She jolted into silence, and he was left feeling mean. But the jibe had been directed as much at himself as her. Okay, she'd been chatting about puddings non-stop for the last hour and forty minutes, but it had been washing over him like a gentle stream whilst he mulled over more important stuff. Like why he was comfortable listening to her giving detailed instructions for making an arctic roll. And why had he'd ended up talking about his family, when he never did. And how the hell he was going to get her into bed.

'Maybe next time we'll bring the limo... and the chauffeur.'

Why had he just said that? When had he ever made promises he wasn't going to keep?

Looking across at her now he knew he'd been right to leave the chauffeur at home. If his hands hadn't been on the wheel tonight, he'd never have kept them off her.

'Fancy a moonlit walk?'

He hadn't meant to ask that either, but somehow now he could see the house approaching he didn't want to get back, not this early, not yet.

'With these shoes?'

He'd already pulled the car off the drive.

'We don't need to go far.' He'd grabbed his parka off the back seat, and was already out of the car opening her door, hauling her out, wrapping his coat around her.

'It's so clear, and the moon's so bright.' Her muffled words came from somewhere inside the hood of his coat.

He grabbed her hand, and started to pull her across the grass with no clear idea where he was taking her. The truth was, his thought processes had been blurred all evening. Sitting opposite Shea in a skin tight dress with an achingly scooped neckline, he'd had a non-stop hard-on of the decade, which had left very little blood for brainwork.

'Don't worry about your shoes, I can get you some more.' She was warm against him now, tugging on his arm unevenly. 'Do you need me to carry you?'

'Don't be silly! You just need to walk a bit slower, then I can...'

'Overruled! Executive decision!' He bent down, scooped her up, breathed in her heat and ran.

She was kicking, squealing, laughing, squirming against him. 'Brando, stop it, put me down! This so isn't fair. Seriously, if you don't put me down I'll probably be sick...'

'Okay, you win.' Breathless. When was he ever breathless? He could sprint for ten miles and not be breathless. Slowly, reluctantly, he dropped her feet, set her on the ground again, her bum cranking his erection off the scale as she bumped him accidentally on the way down. 'Here, lean on this tree.'

He took her shoulders in his hands and felt a shiver convulse through her body as he pushed her back against the wide trunk. He knew he shouldn't be doing this. She was too good to take down to his level, whatever she'd done to him yesterday. Thoughts of that had kept him rock-hard all day, but a niggling part of him suspected he should be getting his bad man sex-for-kicks elsewhere. Yesterday he'd had Shea pegged as a hard-nosed gold-digger he was hell-bent on taking down. But everything he'd seen since suggested she was a lot less tough than he'd thought. God knows what she was doing here.

'Look over my shoulder, see if you can count the stars.' Reaching past the fur trim of her hood, he tilted her chin, felt her breath, hot and uneven, on his wrist. It was as ragged as his own. He tried to resist the desire to grind his length against her pelvis.

'So many stars... they remind me of a pavlova with sparklers I had on my ninth birthday.'

He'd promised himself he'd let her dictate the pace, do the asking, if there was any to be done, as if that made it any more right, but the crazy way his body was burning right now meant that rational thought and self-control were heading out of the window.

'Pavlovas with sparklers! Jeez! One more mention of puddings, and I promise I won't be responsible for my actions!'

She was looking straight up at him, biting her lip, as another judder racked her body. The merest mention of a dessert, and she'd risk the full brunt of his lust.

'Although crumbled chocolate brownies and ice cream also...'

He drew a long breath of resignation. He couldn't say he hadn't warned her.

* * *

'...look good with sparklers.'

She put it down to some lust driven blurred mind aberration. The words were out before she could stop them. She held his gaze, daring him to do his worst, waiting, longing for his mouth to come crashing over hers.

But it didn't.

Instead he dropped a hand to her breast. One thumb scraped across an aching nipple, one bolt of pleasure turned her legs molten. Excruciating. She heard her own moan before she knew she'd made it.

Then he was winding his fingers up the inside of her leg. She quivered uncontrollably as he reached her stocking top. His thumb on the skin of her thigh sent a flurry of electric shocks zithering through her. Wired with lust, she parted her legs, aching for his touch, already throbbing with need. One finger hooked back the silk of her knickers, one gasp from her as he parted her, one choking cry as he grazed her clit, catapulted her need skywards.

'Use me, use me right now!' She hoped her low groan was imploring enough to goad him into action.

An instant, and he'd unzipped, another he'd ripped open a condom packet with his teeth and rolled on protection. An easy tug raised the hem of her dress, then he'd lifted her leg, flicking her knickers aside.

'So ready...' His voice was gruff, roughened with arousal.

One thrust. One exquisite, velvet slide, deep, intense and desperate, sent her to heaven. Grabbing his hair, his shirt, ripping her nails into the contours of his back, she writhed as he pounded her, pushed her, forced her, filled her with pleasure building like an unstoppable tidal wave.

Fast, and furious, she was choking now, fighting for air, one final surge fired her through oblivion, span her out the other side to a cascading, glorious, endless, tumbling fall. Halfway down, she heard his own vibrating, animalistic tremors and knew he was right there, falling with her.

* * *

Pink shrimps, she'd let it happen again. And how.

95

They walked into the light of the porch, and Shea grimaced as the latest wave of shame swept over her. She was following Brando through the back door on tip toe, trying to be exceedingly quiet so as not to disturb anyone, not that there was anyone there, trying to pretend that what had just happened had happened to someone else, not to her.

As he led the way into the kitchen she pulled out the clips from her tangled hair, dislodged a twig and tried to smooth the crumples out of her dress, noticing that he looked no more dishevelled than usual. What else could she expect from a guy who carried condoms everywhere? And what the hell had got into her? When exactly had she become wild and sex-crazed, begging for it from a man like him?

'No need to look so guilty.' He shot her a grin, which made him look way more playful than the hard-nosed player he was. 'We're old enough to have sex in the park if we want to.'

The way she flinched at the word 'sex' only seemed to amuse him more. There was something raw about the way the word sounded when he said it, and the resonance left her trembling. It wasn't the idea of sex in the park which shocked her, but simply that sex with him was so thunderous and raw and explosive. Like nothing she'd ever known. *The sheer animal ferocity blasting away her better judgement, blitzing those guilt qualms.*

He crossed to the fridge, laughing as he opened the door. 'Hot chocolate? It'll warm you up, even if you don't need the endorphins from the cocoa.'

After what she'd just experienced she suspected she had endorphins to last for the next ten years. She watched him saunter around the tiled floor, relaxed as he heated the milk, laid-back as he collected the mugs, dark and achingly beautiful as he stirred in the chocolate, his full-on masculinity seeming somehow incongruous in this domestic setting. Her heart flipped uncomfortably. *Oh jelly beans.* Definitely needing a bit less of the beautiful, and a lot less of the aching.

'Fancy a shortbread with your drink?' He tossed a packet of biscuits from one hand to the other, and slapped them onto a tray.

Shortbread? Who cared about shortbread? Right now she could happily have devoured him. Whole.

Again!

Her eyes fixed on the indentation at the base of his throat, slid down to where she could see a smudge of chest hair, as she imagined undoing his buttons and peeling off his shirt, tasting the planes of his hard, perfectly-muscled torso, carrying on downwards...

She swallowed hard. Pulled herself together.

She'd always professed indifference whenever her housemate Ellie enthused about mentally undressing guys. After the tree-shaking orgasm she'd just had, she should feel satiated, but it only seemed to have made her want more.

Longing to rip off his clothes and ravish him? Really not a good place to be.

Not with a man like him. Not here. Not now. Not ever.

'I'll take that as a yes for the shortbread then!' His deep voice resonated, shook her back to consciousness. 'Come on, open the door for me, and we'll go upstairs.'

Chapter Seven

REAR of the year. Impossibly broad shoulders. And a tray of hot chocolate. One tiny clue that he might, after all, have a human side. Step by step, she promised herself she was hardened to each of these, as she followed him up the stairs in silence. He only spoke as they reached the door of her suite.

'Still an hour and ten to run on the clock I reckon.'

There it was. As expected. She could hear the swagger in his voice. Calm, cool, confident Brando Marshall. Homing in to get his way.

And dammit that her body was thinking exactly the same.

Nice try. She gritted her teeth, determined, decided. 'Thanks. But I don't think so.'

'Fine. Whatever.' He turned quietly, impassive. 'I'll say goodnight then.'

Then he held out the tray towards her, and with one crestfallen look he floored her.

Because instead of seeing Brando, she was looking at a small, vulnerable boy. One it was impossible to say "no" to.

* * *

'You know that the sex against the tree didn't count, don't you, even though you did get hot chocolate straight after?'

Brando was stretched out on the rug in front of the fire in Shea's bedroom, next to his empty mug, idly folding a sweet wrapper. 'Admittedly I *was* more involved in the sex than when you jumped me, and it was great, but I didn't kiss you, we kept all our clothes on and it was over way too fast. Proper moving-on sex requires you to be naked, unresisting and pleasured at length, by someone who knows how to deliver. That's the only way it works. And incidentally, you're unlikely to find anyone who delivers as well as I do.'

Sure of himself, or what? *With the goods and the talent to back it up.*

She sighed as he looked up at her with that triumphant grin she was getting to know too well. Vulnerable boy had legged it pretty fast then. Not that she minded. There was something comfortable about this version of Brando, lounging on her bedroom floor like some rumpled sex-god, with his shirt out and his boots kicked off, that made for a perfect moment. She was unlikely to have another like this, so she might as well savour it.

Seize it even.

After what she'd done the last twenty-four hours, would once more be so bad? She was aching to touch him again. Maybe he *was* right. Once more, properly, might be just what she needed.

Let him take her. *Then* move on. If only she dared...

Sherbet fountains!

She tried to get a grip! Her heart was jolting hard enough to make her feel sick. Had he just said that sex with her was great? She tried not to feel ecstatic about this, and failed.

'You wouldn't be about to offer your services again now, would you?' She gave him a hard stare, tried to keep the laughter out of her own voice, and mentally berated whatever part of her body was sending ripples – or would that be seismic waves? – of anticipation through her.

He flicked the folded wrapper, sent it spiralling into the air, and snatched it back again, neatly.

'It could be arranged...'

She watched him press the wrapper against his lips, narrow-eyed and pensive. Foil and teeth. How was that familiar?

She reeled as the penny dropped.

'Bloody hell, Brando! That's a condom you're throwing around, isn't it?'

'It might be...' Unrepentant. He flashed her the wickedest smile. 'Bad guys like to come prepared!'

'You are so beyond the pale!' She aimed a random kick at him but missed. 'And you are so in trouble!' She knew nothing this man did should shock her. Who else would lie on her hearth rug uninvited, throwing a condom around?

'Did you just try to kick me?' Even as he made his indignant enquiry he closed one outstretched hand around her ankle.

One sharp pull, and she slid off the chair where she was sitting, and landed with a resounding thump beside him on the floor. A bump that should have been big enough to knock some sense into her...

Except now she was on her back, he'd pinned her wrist to the floor, and his face was over hers, deliciously close. Close enough for her to feel his hot breath, shuddering onto her cheek, close enough for her to count every beautiful eyelash, the smoky flecks in his eyes, to see him swallow hard.

He was coming down, excruciatingly slowly.

She bit her lip, found she'd lost the ability to breathe. Noticed a tiny nick of a scar in the stubble shadow on his upper lip. Then his mouth landed on hers, and she tasted him, dark and sweet, and earth-shattering. She surrendered then, gave in to his velvet tongue. A reckless desire pulsed through her as he plundered her mouth. He drew her in, made her want to give him as good as he was giving her. She began to kiss him back, to tangle with him, grabbing his hair with her free hand. Fighting was good. Fighting let her keep control.

She slid a hand under his shirt, buried her nails into taut muscle until he shrugged away.

'Playing dirty?' His gruff growl reverberated across her cheek. With one tug of her arm, he'd flipped her over, undone her zip. Another tug, and he'd peeled her dress over her head, and she felt the burn of carpet on her spine as he tossed her to the floor.

Thank sherbet Ellie had insisted she bought matching underwear.

He leaned back and surveyed her, a lazy smile playing across his sensuous mouth. 'Nice work, Shea perfect-in-every-way. How did you guess I liked stockings?'

Her eyes slid to the bulge that was threatening to burst through his chinos. Holding her gaze, she lifted her foot slowly, planted her heel firmly on the hard ridge of his erection, watched him jack-knife. She wasn't up for scrutiny, she wasn't up for slow, but, whoa, she was up for touching him.

'Lie down Marshall, I'm going to take your trousers off.'

'Or else?'

She applied a sharp pressure with her heel, watched him wince, close his eyes. Rubbing the ball of her foot along his shaft, she saw his head drop sideways.

'Stop that!' He gave a low moan. 'I mean it, you've no idea...'

'Hurting?'

'No, idiot, you're going to make me come.'

She pulled her foot away like lightning, then brought it back achingly slowly. Holding it an inch away from him, she gave him one last teasing nudge. 'Sorry! It just felt really nice.'

'No, no need for sorry, but just take it easy. You make me very...'

'Very what?' She twisted up, knelt in front of him.

He'd thrown his shirt off, looking at her with blurry eyes. 'Over-excited.'

She hooked her finger over the edge of his chinos, ran it along until she met the skin of his tip, hot and taut. Heard him gulp, groan again, as she tugged at his fly.

'Wait...' It was more of a murmur than a word, muffled, as

he deftly peeled down the edge of a lacy bra cup and circled an aching nipple expertly with his tongue. She shuddered, forgot about zips, forgot about everything except the white hot pleasure which effervesced down her body to form a molten pool between her legs, and rendered her helpless. Then he took her nipple into his mouth and sucked hard, and she thought she was going to die. Teasing, biting, playing.

He brought his thumb to graze the other nipple.

She shook her head, trembling, moaned in protest. 'Both – I can't breathe.'

She parted her knees, dug her fingers into the flesh of his biceps, arched towards him; her whole body was crazy, pulsing, vibrating. Nudging her hip bone against his stomach now, she lifted a leg, blindly seeking the jutting mound of his erection, desperate to find it, rub it, force it against the sticky, throbbing ache between her legs.

That was good – good enough almost to...

One, two, three pushes, and a rush of pure chaotic pleasure erupted through her, and she heard her own feral moan, echoing, distant, beyond the ocean rush in her ears. And then he was holding her, steadying her, as she gasped through the blur of aftershocks.

Only the brush of his rough jaw against her cheek some time later stung her back to life, and the thrust of his erection against her stomach sent new flutters of desire spiralling through her. With fingers that fumbled against the straining fabric, she undid the buttons of his fly. He stood up, turned to throw off his chinos and boxers. The naked view of the most beautiful bum in the world ever, made her catch her breath. Tight. Delectably curved. She closed her eyes as he turned back again. She'd seen his front view before, and he'd been big, but then he'd been sitting down, on an office chair. She opened her eyes, a crack at a time to take him in standing.

Pink shrimps! Although on second glance, that definitely wasn't the right thing to say here.

And pheromones. The scent of pure male, mixed with the sex they'd had before, whacked her heart rate to pounding.

'Wow...' She couldn't hide her admiration, or her wide eyes. Huge, awesome, massive. What Ellie would refer to as an XXL. She bit her lip, sucking away the saliva that had rushed into her mouth.

'There's only one place to take anyone as sexy as you, and that's bed!'

She heard his animal growl, caught her breath as her chest constricted in pure panic. *Bed? Who said anything about bed?* She stalled for a second.

'Hey, Mr Conventional!' She steadied herself, regained control. Slipping off the silky scrap of her pants, she tossed them aside. 'Bed's for boring people, and we are so not boring. Lie on the floor...please...now...'

Luckily for her, he was one compliant man.

Sheathed and ready. Most impressive. Another glance at what was on offer rebooted her desire dynamo, then he was down and she was astride him. One last coherent thought, rasped hot in his ear, in gratitude for the exquisite pulse of pleasure that rocketed through her as she found his length. 'Bed's for later...'

And then he was grazing her uncovered nipples mercilessly as she rode him, fingers ripping into his shoulders, taking every incredible inch of him, thrashing, wanting, needing, tearing. Then all hell broke loose, she heard herself scream, heard his deep groan as he went with her, and she thought she might die from the whole glorious explosion.

* * *

He raised himself up on one elbow to watch her as she pulled the lace bra cups back over her breasts, fiddled with a stocking top. Twisted his mouth thoughtfully.

She was ready for him. Might almost have read his mind. 'I suppose you're going to tell me that didn't count either?'

He gave a shamefaced grimace. 'Didn't meet the criteria at all – you still aren't naked, it was still too fast.'

No need for her to know that when he wasn't doing fast and hard, he was the king of long and slow. She was so real, her need so immediate, she had him wired like a powerhouse. Each time she'd demanded a fast finish he'd gone for it like a National winner. Three times now. And each time there had been pure, raw pleasure, like he'd never known. And he was already up for more.

He sprung to his feet, dragged on his chinos, and looked at his watch. 'By my reckoning, we still have ten minutes left.'

'But you're leaving anyway?' Her crestfallen expression spoke volumes.

'Hell no. Just off to get condoms.' Grins seldom came more wicked than the one he sent her now. 'I seem to remember someone suggested bed later?'

And he belted out the door, leaving her to pick up her jaw.

* * *

Brando woke in the early hours with a telegraph pole of an erection, and the unfamiliar sensation of a soft pillow under his cheek. *Crikey, he was in a bed.* That was a first. How long since he'd done that? Plus he'd woken up, which meant he must have been sleeping. And soundly too by the feel of it. What the hell? He stretched a tentative arm across the bed.

Oh no.

There was a drowsy groan, a soft warm body rolled against him. He went rigid as a sleep-heavy arm flopped onto his chest. A trickle of cold sweat meandered down his neck.

'Jeez... Shea?' At least that explained the erection. As for the rest, he *never* made the mistake of sleeping with a woman. *Dammit.* 'Got to go!'

He'd shrugged off her arm, made a muttered goodbye, catapulted out of the bed and was halfway across the sitting room before he remembered. *Clothes.* He banged to a halt, groped for the light switch, then zigzagged round the room, blinking, snatching up the strewn items. He'd blown this one good and proper. Great evening, but leaving five hours too late. One last shoe. He bent for it by the coffee table and froze – a chain and a wedding ring, lying oh-so-innocently.

His heart jolted up to his throat and a bolt of anger made his head pound.

Damn the woman, with her wedding ring and her fire-raising body.

He was out of here.

* * *

'You mustn't mind Brando. He hasn't had it easy.'

Mrs McCaul passed Shea a stack of towels, and she put them on the shelf.

'I know. Edgerton would have been a huge responsibility for anyone at the age of twenty.'

Mrs McCaul's answer to Shea asking if there was any organising she could help with had been to take her along to help tidy a linen cupboard, and this morning Shea was desperate enough to take any distraction she could get.

'There were other things too.' Mrs McCaul's voice dropped, ominously.

Shea grimaced. She didn't want details. She was grateful to Mrs McCaul for giving her a job to do, even if it was patently unnecessary, given they were sorting out a cupboard which was perfectly organised to start with, but she'd been hoping to wipe Brando out of her mind, not discuss him. She'd been so relieved when she discovered he'd left early for London, and spared her the huge embarrassment of waking up in bed with him. Even now she was finding it hard to handle the triple shivers that gripped her whenever she thought about last night. First, a shiver of horror at what she'd done, followed by double aftershock shivers at the recollection of the pure rip-roaring pleasure of it all. Hoping she had concealed her latest wobble behind a towel, Shea looked back to Mrs McCaul, who was waiting for her attention to continue.

'Though you should know all about facing things when you're young, as you were widowed so young...'

Shea lurched. The towel she'd been folding fell in a heap on her feet, and she clasped her hand to her mouth, suddenly fearing her breakfast was going to follow it onto the floor.

All she needed.

On top of the shame of last night, her secret wasn't secret at all. Mrs McCaul knew about Greg. And suddenly this wasn't a refuge where no-one knew about her past, where she was immune from the pitying glances. She was back in a place where people had preconceptions and expectations. How she hated the way people reacted to the twenty four year old widow, not to her.

That was exactly what she'd been trying to escape from when she wrote her postcard. Wives, and weddings, two no-go areas for her, and she'd unexpectedly crashed into the room whilst her friends were up to their necks in both. And somehow, that evening, once they'd got over the shock of her unexpected arrival and they'd stopped cringing with guilt and come clean what they were doing they'd all had a laugh. Just for once they hadn't tried to wrap her in cotton wool, and she hadn't felt like they were tiptoeing around her. She'd had five wonderfully normal minutes. Which was why she'd grabbed at that perfect opportunity to show her friends she was ready to move on, to prove to them she was tough enough, healed enough. Up for a fresh start. No more walking on eggshells.

Not that it had been that easy at home. Even after the postcard evening things hadn't changed hugely. But when she'd come to Edgerton it had been blissful to be where nobody knew. Beyond blissful. She should have known it couldn't last, that the luxury of being seen just for herself and not for her past could only ever be temporary.

'I didn't know you knew.' Her voice wavered, despite her attempts to anchor it. That was it then. And with no work to do either, there was no point in prolonging her stay.

'Don't worry, I won't tell Brando. Bryony thought it best to tell me.' Mrs McCaul sounded concerned. 'I think that's why you can understand Brando. You're good for him and he knows it. I've never seen him comfortable like...'

Shea cut in quickly and decisively, with a hint of desperation. 'I won't be staying, I'm sorry. I have to be busy. There's nothing for me to do here.' She sent Mrs McCaul a smile to reassure her she wasn't responsible. 'Perhaps when we've finished the linen cupboard we can ring Bryony and make arrangements for me to leave?'

Chapter Eight

The last thing Brando expected as he burst through the front door at Edgerton the next evening was to bang head-on into Shea, suitcase in hand.

'And where the hell do you think you're going?'

She shot him a smile so distant it froze him. 'I'm leaving, on the helicopter you've just arrived on. Bryony arranged it.'

For a moment, his skull felt like it was going to explode. He'd just spent two days gnawing the heads off his staff in London, two days unable to see beyond her face etched on his brain, two days while his body baulked in frustration. One breath of her, and already he was feeling better. There was no way he was letting her go, not until this thing was burned out. Not until he was done.

'Not so fast!' Damn Bryony. Damn this woman. Damn the way she pulled him. 'You can't run out now!'

'Oh, yes I can! I came to put my organisational skills to good use. There's clearly nothing for me to do here. So now I need to go.'

Snappy. Cold. Decided. He'd see about that.

'We aren't finished. Nothing's finished. You've hardly started.' He was floundering. He flinched as he heard the note of desperation in his own voice.

'Rubbish, Brando!' Her voice fell. 'Even the attics here look like a tidy obsessive was already there. You don't understand. I can't *not* work. If I'm not busy I...'

Good. She had too many pre-occupations of her own to notice his state, his need.

And she was wrong. He did understand, only too well. *She* needed to work, like *he* needed to run. To block things out. And after he'd run, he worked. And then he ran again. So that was it. His mind flashed back to her need to move on. Some guy must have cut her up good and proper. A flame rocketed through his gut. Fury? Jealousy? Why the hell was he jealous of some random guy for being with a woman he hardly knew?

His mind raced, as he racked his brain to find her a job, some justification to stay.

'Fine! You'll have to sort out the ballroom then!' The words were out before he could stop them.

Damn it.

When he'd closed it fourteen years ago, he'd vowed never to open the ballroom again. Ever. He tore his fingers through his hair in frustration. Whatever desperation had driven him to open it, it couldn't be good. 'Put that darned suitcase down, we'll go and get the keys from Mrs McCaul.'

In three strides he'd reached the office and burst in on his surprised housekeeper.

'Hi, stating the obvious here, but I'm back!'

Mrs McCaul looked up from her work at the desk, and surveyed him with an expression of satisfaction.

'Grace us with your presence twice in a year we're dancing, twice in a week, we're picking ourselves up off the floor.' She grinned past him to where Shea was arriving in the doorway. 'I know you like to keep us guessing, Brando, but luckily for you, this time I guessed right. There's a fire in your room, and there's a cold supper ready for you in the fridge.'

He glossed over the fact that she'd anticipated his arrival more than he had.

'Great, thanks. And Shea will be staying on too.' He noted Mrs

McCaul's affirming nod. 'She's going to sort out the ballroom, so we'll need the keys please.'

Mrs McCaul's eyebrows shot skywards in astonishment as he said the word "ballroom", but he didn't acknowledge the fact. She crossed to the filing cabinet and pulled out a set of keys. She sent a satisfied smile in Shea's direction as she pushed them towards Brando. 'That should give you plenty to do whilst we're away in London!'

He snatched up the keys, pushed them into his pocket with a grimace, and turned to usher Shea out of the office. A slight brush of his thigh against her bottom zapped his simmering lust into overdrive. Shielding his growing erection, he shot a parting smirk over his shoulder at Mrs McCaul as they left. 'She's going to have a very busy time, I guarantee. Enjoy Mamma Mia! See you Tuesday!'

If he was putting himself through the hell of revisiting that ballroom, he was going to make damned sure he made it worth his while. Whatever this crazy heat was with Shea, he needed to burn it up, put it behind him, and quickly. *Starting the moment he got her up to his room.*

* * *

'So, I can carry you, or your suitcases?'

He leaned nonchalantly on the banister, determined not to show how quickly he needed to bundle her upstairs and rip off her shirt. 'Sorry I can't manage both.'

'Neither's necessary.' Avoiding his eye, she bent to pick up her cases. 'I'm perfectly capable of walking upstairs, and I *always* carry my own luggage.' She was so stiff, it was a wonder she didn't break.

'Not this time, you don't!' Before she could react, he had snatched the cases from her, and bounded towards the stairs. 'Race you to your room!'

'I'm not playing, Brando!'

No surprise there then. Ignoring her stern shout, he carried on

110

climbing, determined to ensure that by the time she reached her room, he was already safely inside. As she drew to a halt behind him, he turned, and with one neat lunge he'd hooked her towards him. Suffocating her loud complaints, he bent and captured her open, protesting mouth, ravenously, with his own.

Hot, sweet, deep.

The taste of intoxication set his already kicking heart belting against his chest, and a bolt of pure lust came to a burning halt in his groin. His attempt to staunch his out of control erection by burying it in the warm curve of her stomach failed, but was answered by the taut thrust of her breasts against his chest. He traced a path across the soft nape of her neck with deft fingers, fumbled through the twists of her neatly clipped hair. Two pins, a shake, and her curls were freed, tumbling in a riot around her shoulders.

'No, Brando! Stop!'

She wrenched away, leaving a gaping chasm where her mouth had been, the hard-on of the century groaning against his jeans, and a roar of frustration ripping through his chest.

'Something wrong?'

She eyed him, aghast.

'You can't just start this, not again. Last time was a one-off. I thought you knew that?'

The unexpected words doused him, like a bucket of cold water. What the hell was she here for if not this? What else was there?

'You are joking?' He rounded on her, his lip curling in a sneer of disbelief and disgust. 'Why stop? You were enjoying that as much as me.'

'I chose you because you were a playboy – guaranteed to play once and move on. You can't come back for more! That wasn't the deal.'

He reeled. Reeled because she was right. He *never* did repeats. Until now. Not until this upstart of a woman had dropped into his life, turned his rules upside down and shot his libido into

111

orbit. He felt a niggling tickle as his left cheek muscle twitched. He narrowed his eyes, contemplating his strategy. Whatever his initial intentions, she'd wormed her way under his skin. But only for now, and it didn't worry him. He was a hundred percent confident it would be over, as soon as, and the only way forward was to hammer it out. He just had to smother his outrage, and convince her of that.

'Some fires take longer to burn out than others. A couple more times should be enough to finish it.' He shot her a rueful grin. 'The five hour rule doesn't always work you know, and hell, we might as well enjoy it whilst it lasts!'

He liked his sex hot, but even he knew it didn't usually come this sizzling.

Bingo! He gave a sudden sigh as the tension in his shoulders eased. Why hadn't he realised before? This was all about the spectacular sex. The only reason he was chasing it was the incredible scorching heat. Nothing more.

She lowered her eyes. Shut him out altogether.

'We'll see.' Quiet. Clipped. Dismissive.

'I'll take that as a maybe then.' Another grin, designed to be winning. Another thought. 'Remember no-one back home will ever know what goes on here, so long as you don't parade it when the film crew is around.'

Irresistible.

Hell, he didn't usually have this trouble. When had he ever had to work this hard? Quite simply – never.

'So, if that's all, I think I might settle down with a book...' She looked pointedly in the direction of the door.

So she was giving him his marching orders?

Nice try. Not so fast. 'How about supper?'

'Thanks, but I ate earlier.' She was still refusing to meet his eye.

Dammit. She was blocking him. He had an erection resembling the Empire State Building, and no chance of pushing things to their logical conclusion if he was in another room. And who in their right mind would want to sit and read a book? He switched his brain onto fast forward.

'Why not come and take a look at the ballroom then, if you're so obviously at a loose end?' He watched her hesitation, hoping his casual, throwaway tone hid the fact that this was the last thing he wanted to do.

He'd been dreading going there, even in the morning; the thought of the memories it was liable to disturb sent frozen chills spiralling down his spine.

But if it was that or nothing...

'It's an idea.' She took a deep breath, raised her eyebrows, if not her head.

A chink of light! Capitalise!

'Great! Grab a coat, it'll be cold down there.'

He tried not to think of the ghosts that were waiting for him there, and concentrated on following every squish of her bottom with his eyes as she crossed the room. She picked up the parka he'd bought her from the sofa and unfolded it. He noticed the cashmere cardigans he'd bought her were there too, neatly piled.

'You weren't taking those with you then?' So much for his assessment of her as grasping.

She shrugged, dismissively. 'They didn't feel like mine to take.'

He sniffed. Felt his heart flip as she flicked her tongue over her lips, eyes still downcast. Dammit. She'd just thrown him again.

He dragged the keys from his pocket, tossed them in the air nonchalantly, snatched them back, and gave her shoulder a nudge ten times more playful than he felt.

'Come on then. Let's go and have fun!'

Not.

Suddenly this didn't feel like an easy game. But he knew now he'd come so far he'd be playing it to the end.

* * *

'Enough chaos for you?'

Brando's voice rang out harshly, as icy as the air in the lofty ballroom. He clicked the bank of light switches and the legion of glittering chandeliers rippled into life.

'I guess.' Shea's eyes widened in disbelief as she advanced into the room. She wasn't quite sure what had prompted this unexpected visit, but then with Brando she was never sure of anything. He was only predictable in his unpredictability. And he was making her unpredictable too. Right now, she should have been on a helicopter heading away from him, as fast as she could. But she wasn't. She was still here. Asking herself what the hell she was playing at, she stifled an involuntary shiver as she took in the dusty sea of upturned chairs and tables, empty bottles, and yanked her parka closer trying to stop her teeth chattering. 'I can't say I haven't asked for it. It must have been a heck of a party!'

There were even guitars propped by a makeshift stage.

She picked up a faded streamer, rubbed a cobweb off her nose, fought to get past whatever was chilling her more than the cold, and moved towards where Brando was standing stock still, oblivious, hands in pockets, square jaw rigid, his face milky beneath his tan.

'Are you okay? You look...' She was about to say *haunted* but thought better of it. Before she'd found a more suitable word he sprang forward, grabbed a chair and hurled it away from them. She watched it slice through the air, crash into a speaker stack and splinter into pieces. A glass followed, smashing in an explosion of scattering shards, then another chair.

'Whoah! That's enough!' As she dived to his side, she put a calming hand on his sleeve, but his arm trembled violently beneath her fingers.

The bottle he'd grasped as his next missile hit the floor with an echoing clatter as he let it go, and his face contorted into a bitter grimace. 'This isn't the best place for me.'

Master of the understatement, as usual. She needed to get him out of here. Grabbing his arm, she attempted to steer him towards the door, but he shrugged her off and span out of reach.

'I'm off.' He tossed his ragged explanation over his shoulder as he sprung across the room like an unleashed animal. 'I need to run.'

Before she had chance to react, he was through the door and had disappeared into the night.

* * *

'Fancy meeting you here!'

Shea gave a violent start across the kitchen, almost dropping the milk bottle in her hand. Brando must have crept up on her. His gravelly greeting arrived by her ear.

'Don't do that to people!' Her snapped protest was cut short as she inadvertently stepped backwards, and collided with the damp t-shirt he had screwed up in his hand, and a solid wall of muscle that threatened to blast her cool façade to pieces with flame-thrower efficiency.

Evasive action needed, and fast!

One dive, and she'd skewed across the chequered tiles to safety, and was gasping from a distance at the sight of his lithely muscled torso glistening under the bright lights of the kitchen. He dipped to grab a Coke, and the light from the fridge illuminated the fatigue lines on his sweat-streaked forehead.

She checked her watch as she sloshed milk into the coffee she'd made. 'Have you really been running for three hours?'

'Yep.' He grimaced at her. 'When I run, I push myself beyond exhaustion to the point of oblivion, otherwise I don't feel I've driven myself hard enough. I'm a high energy guy. I like to strive for extremes in every area of my life. That's how I achieve.'

Some mission statement! And an extraordinary level of fitness, which went some way to explaining his phenomenal sexual energy the other night. She blanked that thought as it arrived, but not quickly enough to prevent a flush from spreading across her cheeks.

'And have you achieved oblivion?' Anything to take his attention away from her blush, which was deepening hotly at the thought of the oblivion he'd sent her to. Except his eyes weren't on her cheeks, they were raking up and down her body, hungrily, as if, given half a chance, he'd like to devour her. Pretty much whole. And her treacherous tingling body would so be up for it. Bad, bad thoughts. She shrank back at that one, drew her dressing gown more closely around her, suddenly feeling woefully under-dressed, and watched his throat, vulnerable and exposed, as he threw back his Coke. At least he'd lost his earlier pallor.

He gave a dismissive snort, swiped a forearm across his mouth, and slammed his can down the work surface.

'About before...' His brows closed pensively.

She braced herself. She'd been cursing herself for agreeing to go to the ballroom. She didn't want to hear anything to make her feel more guilty. 'I'm not expecting an explanation.'

'It's better that you know.' He ruffled his fingers through the spikes of his hair, looked down so she could only see the dark rim of his lashes. 'It was difficult for me, because the party we saw back there – my best friend left and was killed in a car crash as he drove home.'

'Oh, shit...' Her voice faded.

The muscle in his cheek wavered, but his voice was low, steady, almost without emotion. 'We were in the band together, that was the last gig we played. The ballroom's been closed up ever since – it's fourteen years now.'

Her stomach plummeted to her knees. She opened her mouth to speak and shut it. She tried again.

'I'm sorry, I didn't mean to cause problems. This is all my fault.'

'No, you mustn't think that.' His voice, low and reassuring, reverberated through her.

He was making her feel better. Just like when Greg died, she'd often been the one who ended up comforting other people. Her mind flashed back to Brando's outbursts. As if his home troubles weren't enough, he'd also lost his best friend. No wonder he was

116

angry.

Oh lordy. Brando and Greg in the same mind space was enough to make her head implode. Except they were from different worlds and different times There was *no* crossover. And if she held on to that thought very tightly she might just keep her sanity.

'That's why you run isn't it?' She turned on him with the sudden realisation, biting back an unexpected rush of affection.

'Partly, maybe. There are lots of reasons why I run.' He shifted, shrugging uneasily under this unexpected scrutiny. 'I didn't intend to tell you about Nick.'

'It's hard to know what to say to help. When things are bad, sometimes nothing seems right.' She shook her head, remembered how trite everyone's comments had sounded after Greg. She resisted the immediate urge to go over and put her hand on Brando's arm. Couldn't trust herself to go so close. A sympathetic smile would have to do. 'Thank you for telling me. It's not always good to run away. Sometimes it's better to face things.'

He bit his lip, studied her through narrowing eyes. 'I could say the same to you.'

A swell of panic choked her as his pointed words sank in. She listened to the dead thump of her heart. Surely he couldn't know about Greg, think she was running away from that? Swallowing deeply she screwed up all the cool she could muster. 'Meaning?'

'Meaning you were about to run away earlier this evening. You were at the door with your suitcase, running away from unfinished business.'

Phew. Was that all? Off the hook. One huge sigh. 'But I'm still here aren't I?'

'Here, but still dodging the issue. Refusing to acknowledge the attraction between us. And that, in my book, is the same as not facing things. Isn't it?'

Off one hook and onto another. Talk about difficult. 'You may have me there.'

'So what to do with the heat then, Shea-rhymes-with-running-away? The fire isn't out yet for either of us, and we both know it. And as you *so* rightly say, we shouldn't run away.' He was screwing her down here, his cheekbones all sculpted in the shadows, his face made even more beautiful than usual by the stress, if that was even possible.

'That isn't what I meant, and you know it.' She gritted her teeth, determined to resist him.

'You don't need to worry. I can guarantee heat this fierce won't last, and it seems a damn shame to waste it. We'll have burned out by Monday, if not before, and then we can walk away. And walking away is a whole lot different from running away.' The dark pools of his eyes, fixed on her face, and turned the base of her stomach molten.

'One night was questionably bad judgement. Another would be too much complication.' Those controlled, measured words sounded as if someone else had spoken them. Obviously her sane self was still in charge of the talking. She needed to get out of here before lust took over.

'Rubbish!' He let out a derisory laugh. 'Mr and Mrs McCaul are off to London for the weekend, we've a whole stately home to ourselves. If you don't do it, you're running away and being a hypocrite. If you do, you'll have a great time and afterwards you get to walk away, integrity intact. So what do you say? From where I'm standing it's a no-brainer.'

She tried to peel her gaze away from those delectable lips of his. That had to be the sexiest mouth ever... she shuddered to think how she ached to have it moving, all over her body. Stamp that out. Thoughts like that were way too dangerous.

'I say you shouldn't play with fire, Brando.'

How had this unbelievable guy moved from dead friends to sex in one breath? Brash didn't come close. She felt ashamed that she was even tempted.

She gave a firm, proud nod to indicate that was the end of it, and marched towards the door.

'Please.'

She stopped, came to a silent halt as she heard his low, grating rasp.

'Sorry?' She twisted to glance at him, and caught him, slumped now against the work surface, transformed from a moment ago. Deflated, bereft. He shifted, lifted his eyes to meet hers, and now she was looking into the eyes of that same, hurt boy she'd seen before. Except this time his eyes, were empty and imploring.

'Please... Shea.' Barely a whisper as he walked towards her with slow, weary paces. He grasped her shoulders, spun her gently. Cupping her face in his hands, he pushed his thumbs along her jaw. 'Don't run.'

She shivered as he brushed his lips lightly across her mouth, her eyes, her forehead. Then, as he buried his head deep into the crook of her neck, she dragged her fingers through his hair, felt his chest tremble first, then shudder against her body. He snatched his breath as she wound her arms around him, burying her fingers in the heaving muscles of his back to hold him firmly. She held him for as long as it took for that powerful, wracking body to still, all the time aching for that desperate, hurting boy.

It was much later when he lifted his head, ground his wet, stubble-rough cheek against hers, rubbed the salty residue on his skin against her lips. Then a moment later she tasted the sweet warmth of his tongue as he slid into a deep, slow, juddering kiss that seemed to drink everything she had to give and more.

* * *

'So, remind me again why you're here Shea?'

He propped himself up on the pillows after a relaxing lunch of champagne and strawberries, and regarded her lazily, ignoring the tiny needle of disquiet which was pricking his euphoria.

It was just that in his book, sex had always been purely for pleasure. He was totally unfamiliar with the concept of sex to make you feel better, but somehow this time sex had done the trick, and there had certainly been a lot of it. Shea was deliciously responsive, and she worked him up like nothing he'd known before, sent him to places he'd never dreamed were possible. Pretty mind-blowing for a guy who thought he'd done it all – hot and turned on didn't begin to cover it. It bothered him slightly that he still hadn't persuaded her to strip off completely, but then who gave a damn about a thong here, or a stocking there anyway. Off-the-scale ecstasy, non-stop since last night was all good to him.

'You know why I'm here.' She stretched languidly, shook her fingers through her curls, which simply messed them more, making her look sexier than ever. 'I sent off a postcard, I'm supposed to be trying out for the position of wife. We both know I'm not going to get the job because I'm way too bossy, not to mention busy, and you don't want a wife anyway.'

'Too damn right I don't.'

He couldn't remember a time when a woman had ever comforted him, made him feel better, and although he was enjoying the benefit, he wasn't entirely at ease with it. And it was increasingly troubling to him that this woman seemed so far from the grasping user he had originally perceived her to be. Stretching out his hand, he ran his thumb down her cheek, to assuage the guilty squeeze in his stomach which thought brought on. One innocent touch, and he registered an immediate buck in his pants; Shea's dynamite effect on his libido, again. 'You still haven't answered my question?'

'I wouldn't be here at all if my client hadn't cancelled – I should have been doing a full home organise for a football coach who took a last minute transfer. I was about to book a holiday when Bryony persuaded me to come here.'

He tried not to acknowledge how the thought of her in some other guy's house made him feel uncomfortable.

'Bryony can be very persuasive.' He knew that to his cost. She was the only person who could wrap him around her little finger, but then that was what little sisters did. He tried not to think about how Shea seemed to have the same ability to make him do what *she* wanted.

'She offered to pay me full salary if I came. I couldn't turn her down.'

'And who's paying that then?' He felt his jaw drop as he anticipated the answer.

'I'd guess you are, if the paperwork was anything to go by.'

He rolled his eyes and gave a grimace which immediately transformed to a grin.

'Jeez – one more living example of Bryony's incredible powers of persuasion.'

So Shea *had* come because of a financial incentive after all. Did that make her more of a gold-digger or not? She wrinkled her nose at him, kicking his erection up a notch.

'I'm sorry, I assumed you knew. Maybe I should've gone to that beach in Bali. If I'd known I was going to have to hang out with a bad tempered sex-fiend like you, I might have thought twice.' She was laughing at him now. 'You have way too many issues to be a husband, you know.'

'And who the hell are you to judge that?' His indignation was a cover. He knew when he was with her he spilled his secrets without thinking. Somehow she had the ability to see right into his soul with her eyes closed. He hoped the directness of his question would make her back off.

'I know from experience. Don't forget I've worked for a lot of guys like you, I can read the signs.' She shot him a knowing smile that made his chest catch, and turned his hard-on to rock. 'Maybe if you dealt with your issues you'd be happier in the long term.'

'Did you just call me a sex-addict?'

'Now you're changing the subject!'

'Admit it, you're as addicted as me!' Maybe he was changing the subject, but then this was becoming an issue for him. When exactly was the heat going to go? Right now it was not only getting hotter, it was also getting more....

'I so am not!'

He let his eyes slide down to her skimpy top, leaned over, pushed his thumb over one tantalisingly erect nipple, as he tumbled on top of her, and brought his mouth down on hers. As he skidded headlong towards yet another bout of glorious oblivion he knew there was something different, he couldn't quite define. Whatever, he was about to have the chance to test it out again.

And he still didn't have a clue about her motives.

Chapter Nine

'That was your mother on the phone. I told her you're tied up until Friday with work, and she can speak to me in the meantime if she wants. And Bryony rang to say definitely hold off on the ballroom and she'll send a guy on Tuesday to film a 'before' shot.'

Brando looked on as Shea rolled over on her pillow, rubbed her eyes sleepily and groaned. He loved the way she was when she woke. An incredibly sexy, rumpled face, hair like a rioting haystack, one foot sticking out of the pile of bedcovers, ready for...

'Not too early for breakfast I hope?' He put his dirtiest thoughts on hold, resting the tray of coffee and croissants on the bedside table. 'I like you sleepy, that way you're less likely to boss me around.'

She sat up, stuck out her tongue, and lobbed a pillow in his direction. 'Have you been running already?'

'Yep.' He ducked, grabbed the pillow to shield the tower of his erection which was making an escape bid through the fly in his lounge pants, and watched her eyebrows rise in query, as he reached for the cafetière. 'Just for half an hour though.'

He'd hardly felt the need to run, but he'd gone anyway. Another morning when he'd woken up beside her, in bed. Another night when he'd slept – in between bouts of sex of course. There'd been plenty of those, and still no sign, as yet, of the heat abating, or the anticipated dwindling of interest. In fact the more he had of her, the more he wanted. He ignored the tick in his jaw which the thought brought on and adjusted the pillow again.

'You shouldn't do that to my mum!'

That whine of complaint may be just what he needed to kick-start the disinterest.

'Although maybe it's best I don't have to cover up what's going on here. She only rings because she cares.'

He snorted. 'There's a fine line between caring and suffocation! Your mother needs to grow up, and give you your independence. You need to train her to see you as an adult.'

She opened her mouth to retort, but then thought better of it. Funnily, he often had the impression she was biting her tongue, holding back, guarding her comments. Not that it mattered. In depth conversation was the last thing they were here for.

'I'll make you a deal...'

'Go on then.'

What was it with her and deals? The fact that she was starting to seem predictable was another good sign. Okay, it meant she'd been round a while, but it also meant he *had* to be closer to the end.

'I agree not to talk to my mum until Friday, if you ring yours.'

He dragged in a breath. If she only knew. Half an idea of the acrimony between himself and his mother, and she'd steer well clear. 'But we haven't spoken for years!'

'My point exactly.' She sat up, inadvertently exposing enough luscious cleavage to make him catch his breath. Hell, he almost flipped the pillow out of the window! She sent him a triumphant smirk, with an underlying grimace of determination. 'Mothers never stop caring you know.'

That burst of an erection proving that his thoughts were anywhere but with mothers.

'I didn't think you were awake enough to order people around.'

She smiled at him ruefully. One raspberry pout, pushing him, demanding.

'I'm always ready to order people round! Even if I'm asleep. You should know that by now.'

Damn. Another reminder of just how long this situation had been going on. He was going to have to work way harder to bring this particular fire under control, and extinguish it once and for all. He slapped the cafetière back on the tray, made a lunge for her ankle, and hauled her towards him, ignoring her indignant squawk of protest.

Too bad. Breakfast was going to have to wait.

* * *

Shea hurried the length of the ballroom clutching her clipboard. As Brando wandered back in, she grinned at him, hitching up the oversized sweatshirt he'd lent her, and fingered a pile of CDs on the table. Weird how her chest tightened every time she set eyes on him. Still breathless in the face of the rugged hunk meets brooding pin-up looks – guilty as charged.

'We've made great progress since the film guy did the "before" shots. Your staff have done a wonderful job clearing up. It's such a lovely room now it's clearer, those tall French windows down both sides make it almost transparent.'

'It certainly had its share of partying back in the day.' He gave a rueful shrug. 'The band hung out here pretty much all the time for two years, when we weren't touring. I only moved to London after the accident.'

'Talking of which, shouldn't you be going back to work?'

He snorted and looked aggrieved. 'This *is* work, or don't you count collecting ten bin bags of empties as working? And you're the one who said I should stay in the ballroom and face my demons. I hope you think this is doing me good, because my back is killing me.'

'Your aching back is down to overwork in another area entirely, and you know it.' She rubbed a sympathetic hand down his spine,

125

trying to forget how easily she touched him now and how the feel of his taut muscles through his t-shirt sent prickles of desire zithering through her, even though it was barely four hours since she'd last had him. 'I'm not talking about here, I meant in London.'

Today was Wednesday. And something about Wednesday had set her alarm bells ringing. If it was Wednesday, what the hell was she still doing in Brando's house?

'They're managing fine without me. I have a very good team in place back there, and it's high time I gave them a break from the big bad boss.'

Not what she wanted to hear.

She should never have allowed herself to come back for seconds, because every day she became more used to him, and more used to being here. And this morning she had woken up with the strangest realisation – she was happy. How long had it been since she felt that? She'd given in to the feeling and was trying to ignore that it made her feel guilty as hell. But how hard was it going to be when this was over?

She watched his profile as he idly flipped through the CDs, spreading them across the table. Insane. No-one had a right to have a jaw-line that beautiful. As for lower down... She sighed, as her eyes wandered lower, catching on the delicious thrusting curve of his fly, and her knees turned to jelly, dammit. Her own fault; she should know better by now.

'Here you go!' His tone was almost triumphant as he waved a plastic case in the air. 'Take a Bullet, Live in Leeds of all places, from 1996. A blast from the past for you.'

She took the CD and examined it. Another photo of the band. She was getting used to seeing Brando looking baby-faced. But was Brando getting used to seeing the photos of his dead best friend beside him? *Shit.* She hoped this was going to help him.

She turned the CD over and baulked at the image on the back.

'Lobster Telephone...'

'Yep, it's Dali.' He eyed her with amusement, one eyebrow

raised. 'And?'

She winced slightly. The memory was sharp in her mind; her friends, their anxious faces raised towards her, as they clocked that she was serious about sending off her own postcard. The way she'd hurtled to her room, grabbed a card from her notice board, hurtled back to the living room.

'You do realise that picture of the phone with the lobster receiver you're sending has a load of sexual undertones?' The words her housemate Guy had said were clear in her mind.

'Trust you to point that out.' She'd grinned at him over her shoulder. 'It's Dali, it's art.' But she didn't even care. She was only doing this to show that she *could*. Nothing else mattered.

She'd scribbled on her card, and dropped it into the envelope Tash was holding out. At the time she was sure what she'd written would guarantee there was no risk that she'd be chosen. All she'd felt was a surge of triumph rising in her chest as she grinned at her friends, and the certainty that she'd just shown everyone she was finally ready to move on with her life.

Maybe not quite in this way though.

'It's nothing important. It was just on the postcard I sent in to Country House Crisis.' Something about this had jolted her heart to a stop.

'Well there's a surprise.'

The slightest tilt of his head, one sardonic smile, a lazy drawl. No clue at all. She had no idea if he was he being serious or sarcastic, let alone if he'd been the one who picked out her card. Thinking about it, it was much more likely to have been Bryony who had decided. A stab of disappointment stung her. Ridiculous. Why should it matter to her who made the selection? Why did it suddenly matter that it was Brando who chose her?

He was staring out of the French doors now, looking across the distant vista of the park, and his mouth twisted into a bitter grimace. 'We'd argued, you know, the night Nick was killed. Just before he left.'

Just like that. Straight out of left field. She closed her eyes, inhaled deeply. It was probably better that he talked about it. She'd started this. She couldn't back away now.

'That's awful.' She watched him swallow, saw his jaw flex as he gritted his teeth, followed the shadows which haunted the hollows of his cheeks. Waiting. Dared.

'You don't blame yourself?'

'Of course I bloody do.' His face contorted, and he spat out the words. 'It was completely my fault and I've lived with that guilt every hour of every day since then.'

She shuddered, hesitated, pulled on a strand of hair, as she struggled to think what to offer him.

'There's no point in ruining two lives. Nick wouldn't have wanted that. You owe it to him to live your life to the full.' She paused, but his only response was an impassive scowl.

'Isn't that what you would have wanted if you had been the one who died?'

He was still stone-walling her.

'Have you talked about this to anyone?'

Third time lucky.

'No. Only to myself – when I run.'

'Maybe you should try. I think it's time for you to forgive yourself. It's the only way you can move forward.'

'You sound as if you know.' He spat the words, his voice acid, accusing, hollow.

Maybe I do.

But none of that belonged here. Here was where she was practising, trying it out, seeing if she *could* live again. This was where none of it mattered, nobody knew, and nothing was for real. She wasn't about to spoil all that with her own revelations.

'I've known people who died, Brando. And people who lived, and pieced things together afterwards and tried to move on. It's the only way.'

'Easy for you to say that.'

She took a shuddering breath, gulped away the sour saliva that had rushed into her mouth, aimed for a lighter tone of voice.

'I was just thinking, given how beautiful the ballroom is looking, maybe you should be thinking of changing some of the other rooms too. I've heard that change is good. There are some lovely sunny spaces at the front of the house, and you'd enjoy it here so much more if we changed them to your taste. We could move out the depressing stuff and make them more funky, get a few new things. It wouldn't take a lot.'

Just for a second he looked as if he wanted to kill her. Then slowly, the stormy furrows on his brow melted away.

'Shea Summers, sometimes you are a complete pain in the butt, do you know that?'

She heard the smallest nuance of humour in his voice as he sidled towards her. He rested his elbows on her shoulders and studied her through narrowed eyes. Just one lazy action sent her heart into overdrive. Then he gave her a half smile, pulled on her tumbling hair, yanked her head back as far as it would go, and held it there.

'You know the punishment for that, don't you?'

* * *

'You do realise my lungs are about to burst! This is so beyond my remit!'

Shea's gasped breaths formed billowing clouds as her protests collided with the cold morning air.

Brando, jogging along the track beside her, stifled a smile as she tugged up her tracksuit bottoms and brushed wild strands of hair off her deep pink cheeks. *Not the only thing way beyond her remit.*

He peeled his eyes away from her bobbing boobs and launched himself into another flip. 'If you complained less, you'd have more energy for running!'

She groaned. 'Putting me in trainers is like putting you in

stilettos!'

'It's our deal – if you insist I've got to come shopping to look for furniture for the house, it's only fair that you suffer too.' He had to admit she was still turning him on, even in this unlikely situation.

She gave a loud, disapproving grunt. 'So have you phoned your Mum yet?'

That put his libido on temporary hold. It was obviously a revenge question and the only answer to that was another question.

'Have you?'

'No. I promised I wouldn't speak to my mum and I haven't. I've been good.' She flashed him a smug smile. 'I keep my promises. How about you?'

'Actually, as it happens, I have.'

He watched in satisfaction as her jaw dropped.

'Oh my! Well done!' She gave him a congratulatory slap on the back.

'She was out, but I left a message.'

'Awww, Brando, I'm so proud of you. You won't regret it – I can't believe things were so bad between you.'

He snorted loudly. She didn't need to know. 'If you'd ever tried living with my step-father you wouldn't be asking.'

'Was he awful to you?' She turned to him, with a wide-eyed concern that made his stomach catch.

'I guess, if I'm honest, he wasn't. Maybe I resented him taking my mother's attention. I was thirteen. I kicked off, that's all' He tried to sound matter-of-fact, head her off.

But this was Shea. There was no heading her off. She was already rounding on him.

'You mean you were jealous?'

Bang! Got it in one. Jealousy. The Achilles heel that had derailed his life, not once, but twice. That fierce need he had to possess for himself, when it came to love, the thing that made him vile, unreasonable, and impossible, whenever he cared.

'I wouldn't say that.' He gritted his teeth, drummed his feet against the ground and shot ten yards ahead of her before he knew, shouting back to her. 'Tell you what, I'll run on, let you get your breath back. See you back at the house in a bit.'

Even from here he could feel her astonished disappointment.

Damn. He didn't wait for a reply. He was already pounding down the road. How had he thought running with her was a good idea?

Jealousy; the reason he could never be with anyone ever again.

And he certainly wasn't going to talk about it.

* * *

'Jealousy is a very destructive emotion, you know.'

Shea tossed that out across the cream leather back seat of the limo, in the hope that it would reach Brando. At least in a car he couldn't run away. Maybe it was going to be hard, but now she'd brought his difficulties to the surface, she owed it to him to talk about them. She knew from experience that burying problems didn't make them go away. If you were brave enough to confront them, at least you stood a chance of getting over them.

He looked up from his laptop, and sniffed irritably. 'Haven't you got an itinerary to organise?'

Damn that his sulking didn't diminish the effect he had on her lust levels. They were still disgustingly out of control.

'Pretty much got that covered thanks.' She grinned at him, and tried to concentrate on plans for the day. 'I got a tip for Bath's hottest shop from my housemate who does interiors. So long as you like the style, we should find everything you need there and minimise your suffering.'

'Just the kind of news I like to hear!'

'So now can we can talk about how jealousy isn't good please?' Priority number one here, after all.

He closed his eyes, exhaled loudly, shook his head distractedly. 'As you obviously refuse to give up you may as well know – the

131

argument I had with Nick before he died was caused by jealousy.' His voice was low, his jaw hardened, his hands clenched into bitter fists. 'If anyone knows about the destruction it can cause, it's me. Don't you think that's lesson enough, without your preaching?'

Oh sweet peanuts! That should teach her. 'I'm so sorry! Putting both feet in it, again! I wasn't judging, I just thought it might be good – to talk, I mean.'

'Don't worry about it. You weren't to know. Here, look online and show me some sofas. I brought the limo so you could do that on the way.'

A sting of unexpected disappointment hit her. *Damn.* Why had she been ridiculous enough to imagine the limo was for en route clinches. Why should she care anyway?

'Trips in the limo will give you practice for later.' She had no idea where that came from other than a need to hit out. 'You've cracked the dating now. You're way beyond your five-hour limit. I'd say you're pretty much all set for a relationship.'

'Why?' He flipped a lazy leg across hers, eyed her with a laconic smile. 'Are you offering?'

Liquorice sticks! Her stomach did a dizzy triple flip. She ignored the out of control skitter of her heart, swallowing hard to quell the fizz.

'No way! I'm entirely not available!' It came out five times louder, ten times more emphatically than she intended.

He twisted his jaw, scrunched up his lips, contemplating her.

'Then I don't understand – what the hell are you here for? I thought you were desperate for a husband?'

Kerching! Home-truth time, it had to be done. 'I'm here because my work had fallen through, I couldn't face going on holiday, and I couldn't bear the thought of having nothing to do. The last thing I want is a husband. I don't even want a relationship.' Her words tumbled out in one desperate gush of honesty.

'I see.' His slow response and impassive frown gave no clue about the level of his annoyance.

'I only played along to challenge you, because I could see you were so against the idea of a wife. It was a wind up, I didn't mean to lie.' She rushed on, shooting him a placating glance, wishing it didn't sound so bad. 'To be honest it was a shock to find you here. Bryony told me you hardly came. She wanted some film footage, I needed to be occupied. It seemed like an ideal arrangement.'

'Well, thank you Bryony.' He shook his head, rolled his eyes, then turned to her with a stare that drilled to her core, tapping his teeth with a finger. 'Sounds to me like your work obsession is like my compulsive running. It takes one to know one, Shea-rhymes-with-play. So what exactly are *you* blocking out?'

She shrank under his scrutiny. A desperate marriage at eighteen to a terminally ill husband who disintegrated while she stood by helplessly. Then four years as a widow, trying to piece her life back together, while everyone danced around her at arm's length, too scared of upsetting her to get near her. How about that for starters?

Poor, sweet Greg, and his brain tumour.

It was no business of Brando's. Even if he had inadvertently helped her take a step towards reclaiming a normal life, there was no way she was letting him rake over her memories. Greg belonged in the other part of her life. No cross over was how she was surviving here. She was keeping the guilt and the betrayal at bay by telling herself that nothing here counted. If Brando knew about Greg he'd see her differently, and that would be certain to change things between them. Whatever it was they were enjoying now would be finished. A judder turned her insides cold, because she wasn't sure she was ready for that. Not yet.

'I'm trying to leave the past behind, you already know that. I'm not up for emotion.' She tried for a radiant smile, struggled for an upbeat note, as she tried to assimilate her shock at that last realisation. 'We're burning out heat here, if I remember rightly. And we both know we'll soon be done.'

'Too right! ' He gave a short, hollow laugh, and sent her a weird look that implied she'd misunderstood him entirely. 'Who

133

the hell said anything about emotion? Grab the laptop and show me some sofas!'

* * *

'Oh sugar! I'm not sure I'm the best person to do this.'

Shea gazed, wide eyed, around the lofty furniture showroom, with its startling array of furniture and accessories, suddenly bemused. 'I'm good at helping you decide what you'd like to keep, what you need to make your home work. I'm not a designer.'

'Hey, you can't get me this far then run out on me! That's not how it works!' His retort was playful, yet chidingly indignant. 'I've already told you a designer makes it too clinical. This time I want to choose things for myself, buy sofas I'm comfortable sitting on and I need your help because you know me.' He shot her a grin he hoped was reassuring. 'I'm not asking you to be Kelly Hoppen!'

He watched her take a deep breath, smooth down that delectably tight pencil skirt that accentuated her curves so perfectly, and visibly pull herself together with a tug of her peplum jacket. He loved it when her confidence ruptured and he caught a glimpse of the vulnerability underneath. When she turned back to him she'd recaptured her radiant smile, and one flash of it sent his stomach into the tailspin he knew to expect now, but still hadn't quite worked out how to handle.

'I guess I was the one who said cushions were more meaningful if they had history. Caught out by my own blarney yet again.' She gave a momentary grimace, and took a monumental deep breath. 'So, bearing in mind that your favourite colour is grey and you have a pathological hatred of florals, let's try out some seats. Whatever we choose, if it makes you want to spend time at Edgerton, it can only be good.'

* * *

'So, not so hard after all, was it Brando?' Her heels clicked as she marched imperiously ahead of him. He had no idea where she was heading, but he was pretty much willing to follow that delectable rear wherever she wanted to take him. 'Sofas for three rooms sorted in fifty minutes. You're a very decisive shopper, I'm impressed!'

'Does that mean I get to eat now?'

He counted the seconds it took her to moan inwardly and roll her eyes. *One, two...*

'We can maybe allow that, so long as it doesn't take too long – build up your strength for the rest.' She flashed him a mischievous half wink over her shoulder.

'You mean there's more?' He gave a mock groan.

'You know there's more. In fact, I'll just check if that same assistant is going to be here this afternoon. He's so helpful, and I don't want to overstretch your attention span.'

He watched her twirl and head off, enjoying the view as she twisted her way back across the showroom. He had no idea how she could walk in heels like that, but he sure as hell liked the way they made her bottom wiggle. She'd reached the pay desk now, was inclining her head, making small neat gestures as she chatted to the guy there. Even from this distance she exuded sex appeal. He tried to take his eyes off her, and failed. As he saw the assistant stretch out a hand, rest it on her shoulder for a second, his heart begin to hammer, his chest tightened like a tourniquet, and a furious burst of adrenalin pulsed through him.

What the hell?

He grappled with himself, resisting the sudden violent urge that seized him.

All he wanted was to race across the store and wrench her away, floor the guy, and grab her for himself. *Crazy time or what?*

He shut his eyes tightly, shook his head. Dizzied. Fighting himself. And the damned realisation that he wanted to possess her. No way was this happening, not to him.

Not now, not ever.

By the time he opened his eyes, his heart rate was subsiding, and then she was beside him again, her hand feather-light on his forearm. Two gasps of her dusky, summer scent calmed him measurably.

'Okay Brando?' Her question fluttered against his cheek.

'Yep, never better!' He forced the ironic words between gritted teeth, giving a disgusted snort as he rammed his hands into his pockets and spun on his heel. 'Come on, hurry up, or we'll be way too late for lunch.'

He cringed inwardly as he heard his footsteps thudding on the pristine polished walkway. He knew he was acting unreasonably, but right now he was beyond being polite. He needed to put the brakes on himself, and hard, before this thing got any more out of control than it already was.

* * *

'Shopping mission accomplished, and I'm still in one piece.' He grinned in her direction across the dimness of the rear seat, as they sped back towards Edgerton.

'Speak for yourself, my feet are killing and I'm exhausted! It was quite a surprise when you insisted on buying up most of the bedroom department too. Your running gives you way too much stamina in every area of your life Brando Marshall.' She slowly eased off one shoe at a time, letting them drop onto the luxurious carpet. As she deftly tucked her legs beneath her, she leaned towards him.

'I like to be decisive. And you forget, I hadn't actually slept in a bed for a very long time. Now I do, the least I can ask for is a comfortable one.'

However much of a shock he'd given himself before lunch, he'd been determined not to take it out on Shea. After all, his short-comings weren't her fault. Plus, he'd spent the whole afternoon rationalising that his over-reaction probably had a lot more to do with him needing lunch than anything else. He tested himself by letting his gaze wander over the contoured shadows of her breasts, up to the soft indentation below her throat, and gave a low, satisfied growl, because there he had the proof. Pure lust, nothing more. All he needed to do was be aware, push on for burn-out as soon as, then get the hell out of here. A dangerous game, but then wasn't he the expert with risk?

He nudged Shea gently in the ribs with his elbow. 'Your mother was not wrong when she told me you had a cushion fetish.'

'Sorry? When was this exactly?' She rounded on him with a mixture of disbelief and puzzled indignation.

'Not sure which day it was. We've been chatting quite a lot – I thought I'd better let her know you were okay, seeing as you haven't been phoning her. Your dad's been playing golf, your sister's bought a stunning dress for the Squash Club winter ball, and the dog ate a whole apple pie to himself yesterday.' He stifled his laughter, tried to sound nonchalant. 'You'll be phoning her yourself tonight anyway, you can catch up then.'

She rubbed her nose wearily, swallowed a yawn. 'You always surprise me, do you know that? I was furious about the ban on phoning my mum at first, but it has been good to have a break. Thanks for keeping in touch for me.'

He stretched out an arm, pulled her towards him, casually, teasing. A bolt of desire coursed through him, as one firm breast pushed against his ribs. She yawned again, dropped her head heavily on his shoulder. *Damn.* He'd brought this car so they could make full use of the space on the dark ride home, and he hadn't planned to sleep. As she wriggled against him, her closeness warming his chest, his irritation melted, but in its place he felt something horribly, achingly protective.

'I'm sorry if I was short with you this morning...'

She murmured in query.

'... about the jealousy thing.' If whatever they had was almost over, he didn't want to leave her thinking he was a complete heel.

He had a flashing vision of his life back in London, life without her, as it had been before and stifled a shudder. It was suddenly important that she knew. 'The argument with Nick, just before he died – I wrongly accused him of trying to steal my girlfriend. That's what we argued about. I saw them together, jumped to the wrong conclusions and went for him. I was insanely jealous, so jealous I couldn't see the truth. It was only afterwards I found out she *had* been cheating on me, but not with him. When I'd seen them together he'd been tackling her about it. He didn't want to tell me what was going on; he'd hoped that talking to her would be enough. But we argued, he left, and the rest you know. I'll always blame myself and my jealousy for his death. If it hadn't been for my jealousy, he wouldn't have left, and he would still be alive.'

'Brando, I'm so sorry.' She rubbed her hand across his head, ruffling his hair, down over the roughness of his jaw. 'Thank you for trusting me enough to tell me.'

Jeez, he'd gone and spilled his guts. Again. Why, he had no idea, despite the fact he'd wracked his brains every time it had happened. He only knew that when he was with her, his secrets came tumbling out. Yet despite the fact he hated every time it happened, it seemed to make things better, not worse. He was feeling better about the past, better about himself, better about the future.

'Is there anything I can do to help?' She traced an idle finger down his cheek, over his lips.

Shutting the hell up about trust might be good.

After last time, he'd vowed never to trust anyone again. Ever.

'Now you come to mention it, feel free to shed as many of your clothes as you like. Naked will be perfect.'

He slid his hand around her waist until he found her skirt button and popped it open. Tugging down the zip, inch by aching inch, her skirt was free to ride up. Then he dragged her to face him, and with one easy lift he'd whipped her on top of him. He let out a low growl as her pelvic bone ground hard onto his already whopping erection, put his hands on her hips to readjust her so he didn't burst there and then. Only once she was straddling him comfortably did he take her face in his hands and kiss her long and deep, and hard.

'Jeez, I needed that!' He broke off, his penis throbbing madly beneath her, forging against his fly.

For a second he fumbled in his back pocket, then he pulled out a foil packet, which glinted in the half light as he flipped it towards her.

'Okay, Shea, I'm waiting, and I'm way beyond ready. Do your worst!'

* * *

'Hey you, how's it going?'

Shea started slightly at the unexpected sound of Brando's voice, and stood up from where she was delving deep into a massive box of home accessories which had arrived that morning, rubbing her forehead with her wrist.

She shot him a smile, feeling suddenly shy.

'I know I like to be busy, but these last few days have been crazy with the house makeover. I had no idea you had so many staff. There seem to be more each day, and they're all so industrious and creative. It's amazing. And we're getting so much done!'

She fished out a cushion from the box and began to remove the wrapping.

'I think you've inspired them, Shea. It's not just in the house, there's a whole army of them out there who run the estate. You've given them a reason to get excited, and they've all flocked to help. It must have been pretty soul destroying to come to work year in, year out, to a house where nobody lived, and nothing changed. I always presumed it was enough for them that I employed them. I never thought about it in those terms before. There are a lot of things about Edgerton I haven't ever addressed, until now, that is.'

'And you're sure you don't mind that the decorators have been called in too? And the carpet fitters and the curtain makers, not to mention the telephone guys? When I suggested changing things, I only meant to make a couple of rooms a bit more like you so you'd enjoy being here more. It's turned into a total blitz – it's as if the whole thing has taken on a life of its own.'

'You have that effect on people.' He gave her a hard stare. 'Or hadn't you noticed?'

Brando talking about people affecting other people was dangerous, given she was trying to block out the effect he was having on her. She hated to admit it, but there was a seismic shift in the way she felt inside, the way she felt when she was with Brando, about Brando. Something was changing, but she didn't dare to face it, didn't want to face it. Even thinking this was too much of an admission. It was good that she didn't have time to think about it, fab that she had so much work to bury herself in. Being rushed off her feet didn't begin to cover it. Just how she liked things.

She rubbed her nose, ignored that comment completely, and carried on. 'Are you sure you don't mind? I hardly see you these days to ask.' It was true. If she needed him for something specific, he complied immediately with whatever she requested, making decisions at his usual break-neck speed, but apart from that he made himself very scarce. She assumed he was working, unless she happened to catch a glimpse of him, as she often did, way in the distance, heading out over the park.

'I've got a lot on.' He sounded dismissive, but he looked quickly away, avoiding her gaze. 'Deals to do, and all that.'

Which told her nothing at all. She noticed the flicker in his cheek, a fleeting expression that might have been guilt. She could hardly tell. He'd seemed strangely distant lately, like he was there, yet not there.

'You'll need a few deals to pay for all this lot! It's a good thing you aren't on a budget!' She aimed for jokey. He mustn't know she'd noticed he'd withdrawn. She had no right to care.

Except he was still there for the sex. The sex was still burning. That night in the car – she went hot all over again at the memory. The purr of the engine, the blur of the night outside, how she rode him, thrashing astride him until they both exploded. Simply remembering his raw anguished shout as he came sent a shudder jiving through her. She had a sudden urge to stretch out her hand, touch him, pull him to her, close this chasm between them.

For just this once she didn't want to wait until after midnight. These days he came to her later and later each evening, almost as if he were avoiding her. She wanted to rub the stubble shadow of his jaw, make him want her, here, now. Arching her back, she gently tilted her breasts towards him.

'You can say that again!' He went on briskly, oblivious to the nipples thrusting towards his face. 'Anything else I can help you with? If not I'd better be off.'

And then he was gone, as quickly as he'd come, leaving her, cushion still in hand, nipples still in mid air, with a heavy ache which began in her throat, and swung like a stone into her stomach.

Sour apples! He'd totally blanked her. She bit back a rush of raw saliva. So this was how rejection tasted? Not good. But two could play at that game, and she'd make damned sure he was the one doing the waiting tonight.

Chapter Ten

It was after one in the morning when Brando heard Shea creep back to her room later that night. He'd kept away from her all day, yet again, not that it made any difference. He'd hoped that by staying away he'd get her out of his system, that he'd be able to stop obsessing about her, but it had only served to make him more desperate, as his already thrusting erection proved.

'I thought you were never coming!' He blustered through, raking his fingers through his hair, about to drag his t-shirt over his head, but one look at her tight expression stopped him in his tracks. 'Something wrong?'

'Nope.'

She kicked off her pumps, flopped onto the bed, her eyes lowered, and his stomach sank.

A one word answer from a female. Ominous.

Careful to avert his eyes from the horribly inviting curve of her breasts, he plumped down beside her. The way she stiffened as he flung a casual arm around her shoulder set his alarm bells ringing loud and crazily.

'Tell me what's wrong.'

He already knew the brush off he gave her earlier was unforgivable, but at the time he hadn't been able to help himself. It had been a matter of self-preservation. For him, the nights were less dangerous. He could think of those as sex, and sex alone. It was how he felt when he looked at her in the day that he couldn't handle.

'If you won't say what's wrong, at least tell me what you've been doing?' Less dangerous territory all round.

'Checking all the last minute details – don't pretend you've forgotten the film crew arrives for final shots tomorrow afternoon.'

'Six hours of last minute details?' He inclined his head in disbelief. He felt her shuffle, turn towards him, and as she raised her face to him, the tears in her eyes made his chest catch. 'I'm sorry. About before...'

'It's okay. It's just I don't seem to see you anymore.' She attempted a half smile, then added a disclaimer. 'Not that I have any right to see you. I know that.'

So this was the girl who wasn't ready for emotion, crying because she hadn't seen him enough, and he was the guy who had sworn he'd never let himself care again, who couldn't bear to see her because it made him know he was caring too much.

What the hell had happened?

'I've been trying to stay away from you.' The words flew out in a rush, despite his best intentions. He couldn't begin to explain how, with him, caring and jealousy went hand in hand, all the way to destruction. Every time. 'It's for your own good. I make bad things happen....'

'If what we're doing is bad, I think I might like being bad.' Her response was barely a whisper. 'I'm having such a great time. You have no idea.'

Her words sent a warm rush flooding through his body. He gripped her shoulder, gently scraped her skin with his fingertips, felt her become malleable beneath his touch. Scratching a nail along the inside of her forearm until she shivered, he nudged her backwards onto the pillows.

Suddenly he knew this was going to be sweet. Achingly sweet. And it was going to be spell-bindingly slow. Because for the first time ever she was going to lie back and let him do *all* the pleasuring.

Without him asking, she was giving him complete surrender.

'Come on.' He heard his own voice, husky, thick with desire. 'I'm going to make love to you.'

* * *

Hitting the office at nine the next morning was a struggle. Shea, still dizzied with a mixture of afterglow and fatigue, attempted to be breezy, as Mrs McCaul went through the list of things to be done.

'So I'll get the team onto final floor polishing in the library and the ballroom, and then move onto a final clean everywhere else. Is that okay, Shea?'

She nodded dumbly as Mrs McCaul's plans floated past her, rubbing her mouth distractedly, hoping her hastily applied lip gloss was enough cover for her swollen lips. Last night had been so... She struggled to define it. Deep? Naked? Mind-blowing? Whatever, it had made this morning *so* unprofessional. The Shea Summers who arrived here a month ago would *never* have turned up for work in this state.

'Then after that it's flowers?' She tried to sound as if she was keeping up, as she dragged her unruly hair back, and recaptured it into another hasty pony tail which still failed to do the job. 'I love the flower part!'

Mrs McCaul carried on bustling about the office, seemingly unaware of Shea's discomfort.

'And Bryony sent this through for you to check.' Mrs McCaul smiled and pushed a piece of paper across the desk towards her. 'It's just your details for the files – I can't think how it's got left until now.'

Shea started as Brando bounded into the office, snatched up the paper, whisked it behind her, and leaned hard against the filing cabinet.

Where the heck had he come from? She'd been counting on a morning without him to try to get her head straight. Last night had been so different.

Too different.

Right now she wasn't sure that different like that had been was something she could handle.

Brando advanced towards her. 'What? Details on Miss Summers? This I must see!'

Damn it! He *had* seen it! In the small of her back, she scrunched the paper in her fist, as her stomach plummeted, her throat constricted. She flinched as he sprang towards her and dropped a light hand onto her waist. She knew she should run, but her legs had frozen. *Crap, crap!* She gasped in his familiar scent. One tweak, and he'd grabbed the paper, and was backing playfully away across the office, waving it triumphantly.

Oh shit! How had she let that happen? Careless didn't begin to cover it.

'Let's see what middle names you've been hiding then?'

Think on your feet...

'I already told you, Pixie Persephone!' She squeaked out the first desperately jokey reply she could, hoping she could brazen it out, that he'd put down the paper, that maybe she could grab it, before he saw...

Too late.

She read the puzzled furrow of his brows, and simultaneously felt her stomach plummet to somewhere round her ankles. The worst had already happened.

'There must be some mistake here!'

Shea, feeling her body flush like a furnace, then turn icily cold, was distantly aware of Mrs McCaul getting up from behind the desk and sliding noiselessly out into the corridor, discretely closing the door behind her.

'Don't worry we'll get it changed as soon as we can. In the marital status box they've put you down as a widow, that's all.'

That's all?

She heard the pulse banging in her neck, a rushing in her ears, felt the strength drain from every pore of her being. For a long time she forgot to breathe.

'There's no need to look so worried, it's not that serious! It's only Bryony's office being slap-dash.'

She hugged her arms tightly around herself, wishing he'd just be quiet.

'It's not a mistake.' She spoke quietly, throwing out flat, dead words that hung in the air. 'The form is right. I *am* a widow.'

Nothing to feel guilty about. Just a statement of fact. She turned to face him, squaring her jaw.

'You are what..?' He stared at her, his brows jagged with disbelief.

'A widow, Brando.' She made her words icy. Sarcasm seemed the only recourse to his hotly accusing tone. 'Widow as in 'I used to have a husband, but he died' kind of a widow.'

There was one aching moment of stillness and then he jack-knifed.

'Well thanks a lot for keeping me informed.' He rounded on her bitterly. 'And when exactly where you planning to tell me this?'

She widened her eyes wildly, totally floored by his antagonistic reaction.

'To be honest – never. It has no bearing on anything, and you had no need to know.'

He turned on her, his face thunderous.

'To be honest? You're standing there talking about being honest. That's a damned contradiction for starters. When I think of all the truths you've forced out of me!'

'I don't recall *forcing* you to tell me anything!'

'Everything we've talked about, and you managed not to mention this!'

'I always tried not to lie about it.' She was eerily calm, carefully measuring her words. A twinge of guilt pricked her as she remembered what she'd told him about her wedding ring. 'And the ring *was* my grandmother's before it was mine.'

'Obviously you don't count lying by omission! I'm sorry, I don't know what rules you play by, but in my book that's as good as lying.'

'I'm sorry you feel like that.'

'Jeez, Shea, and how the hell else would I feel?' He was shaking his head at her vigorously, already backing towards the door. 'I'm going for a run.'

She flew at him fiercely, shaking with anger now, using every ounce of self-control to stop herself from yelling like a banshee. 'A run? Great! Why does that not surprise me? You get a problem, and all you can do is get the hell out of here!' She flung open the door and stood back, making a sweeping flourish with her arm to wave him through. 'Well off you go. I hope you enjoy yourself! The rest of us have work to do!'

* * *

Brando broke off the ear-splitting riff he was ripping out on his guitar, and looked up to see Shea staggering towards him across the ballroom, peering over a huge stack of flower boxes she was carrying.

'Brando!' Her initial surprise hardened. 'I thought you were out throwing yourself off buildings.'

She had a good line in sarcasm, but he wasn't going to rise to it.

'It didn't work, so I thought I'd come here. Pull in some guitar practice.'

It had been fourteen years since he'd picked one up, and it was proving a pretty effective way to rip the guts out of something. Just what the doctor ordered for when parkour failed him, and there was stuff he needed to get his head around.

So much stuff...

Last night, for the first time, Shea had been completely naked. For the first time she had trusted him to take control. *Sweet heaven didn't begin to cover it.* And last night he'd finally admitted to himself there was more to this than lust. Not that he could ever allow himself more than lust. He understood that. Not him, with his jealous streak and the trouble it had caused in the past. And it wasn't as if Shea was exactly up for anything emotional either. But somewhere in the dark, wakeful hours, he'd found some vague, distant hope, that maybe they could work this through. Then this morning's dead husband grenade blew those hopes to pieces. And right now the sight of her sent a corkscrew of pain through his chest that made him want to explode.

As she wavered towards him he put down his guitar. Gritting his teeth, he reined in his wrath. As furious as he was, if he didn't intervene here, she'd drop the lot.

'Give those to me.'

The smell of fresh flowers hit him as he grappled the boxes from her. The faintest overlay of the scent of their early morning love making as she brushed against him made his face fold into a bitter grimace. He slammed the load onto a nearby table.

'I've never heard you play the guitar?' Her voice was small, tentative.

Jeez. And now she expected polite, detached conversation? He gave a dismissive snort, too angry to attempt a reply.

'About before, in the office. Brando?'

So that's what she was here for. Miss Shea-never-go-away would be, wouldn't she?

She was a brave woman for daring to go there, given his whole being was imploding, and for some inexplicable reason he felt like his heart had been ripped out of his chest. He had no idea how she had the nerve to stand in front of him now, all square and righteous.

'What about it?' He stood back, sniffed derisively, folded his arms. 'This had better be good.'

'It's important that you understand – I didn't intend to deceive you.'

'What?' He choked on that one. 'Now I've heard it all.'

Watching her fiddle nervously with her lip, his head throbbed and he knew he should be cutting her more slack. He just couldn't find a way right now.

'I can't believe you're being like this Brando. I didn't tell you I was a widow, because coming to Edgerton was the first chance I'd had to be somewhere where no-one knew about my past. You've no idea what bliss that was.'

He saw a smile play on her lips for a moment, and his heart, obviously still there despite illusions to the contrary, did a double basketball bounce off his ribs. Then her face fell, and made his stomach flip again, because now, although her voice was steady, she couldn't make herself hold his gaze, and her eyes were full of tears.

'For the last four years all anyone has seen me as is a widow. Most people crossed the street rather than face me. The friends who did see me skirted around, always afraid of upsetting me. I entered Bryony's stupid competition to prove to them I was ready to be treated like a real person again. All I wanted was a way back into the real world. Since way before Greg died I've never been seen for myself. Was it such a crime to want to be treated as a normal twenty-four year old? Somehow I hoped you'd be different, that you'd understand. Do you realise, you haven't even told me you're sorry?'

He started as he heard her say 'Greg'. The rest was a blur.

A dead husband with a name. That made him all the more real. He baulked at the way it made his ribs constrict, sending flame-thrower heat roaring through his chest. And as the heat seared through him, he nailed the true source of his rage. It wasn't because Shea had hidden the truth. It wasn't about that.

He was furious, because he was jealous. Jealous of her dead husband.

He shook his head. 'Of course I'm sorry, sorry for your loss, sorry for not understanding, sorry for the whole damned mess. But I fail to see why you would keep something as important as that from me. I can see you wouldn't tell me on day one, but somewhere down the line you could have said. Hell, you had every opportunity.'

He watched a look of wild guilt tear across her face, but when she spoke again her voice was chilled.

'It had no place in our casual arrangement, the arrangement you wouldn't even call a relationship, if you remember. Things were perfect as they were, you had no need to know.'

Did she just say perfect?

'I'm not cross that you're a widow. That damned wedding ring dangling from your neck, I should have guessed.' He heard his own dismissive snort stretch into a hollow, bitter laugh. 'But I'm disappointed you didn't tell me, given what we shared.'

He let his gaze drop, knowing he was lying now. He couldn't be more unhappy about her having a husband, even if he *was* dead. A living husband he could have dealt with, but a dead one was so much worse. A dead husband would never go away, would always be there to claim her love. With his track record of jealousy, he was not the guy to make that one work, when every time he had a fleeting thought about it he choked with rage.

'You're disappointed?' Her voice had an incredulous note. 'Well that makes two of us. And for the record, if I didn't feel so guilty, I'd be bloody annoyed too.'

'You know this changes everything?' He stared at her stonily.

'And that's exactly why I didn't tell you. You saw me for myself, and that was special. I didn't tell you about Greg, because I didn't want that to change. All you'll ever see now when you look at me will be a widow. Just like everyone else.'

Wrong. All I'll ever see when I look at you now will be your dead husband. Guaranteed to drive a man crazy.

Get yourself out of that one, Marshall.

He wanted to pick up the guitar, and smash it to oblivion. Smash every chair in the place. Carry on smashing until the whole room was nothing more than a pile of splinters. But his limbs refused to move.

Her voice cut into his haze. 'Don't worry Brando, a couple of hours and I'll be gone. I'd have left already, but Bryony rang and stopped me. Apparently it's a huge deal for her.' Her chin jutted. 'And by the way, thanks Brando.'

No surprise that Bryony had already heard. Well done Mrs McCaul.

'Thanks for what exactly?' He flung the words at her like darts.

'You made me come alive again, and you showed me I can move on with my life.' She put her mouth close to his ear and breathed the words 'Thanks for being bad with me, Brando.'

The knot in his stomach was flaming, but his blood ran glacial, freezing him to the spot.

For a moment he felt a flutter of warmth as her lips glanced across his cheek, and then she melted away, leaving him with a fast fading scent of summer, and a chasm in his gut like he'd never felt before.

That was so like her. Saying thanks before she left.

Or saying thanks, before he left? Because leaving was exactly what he was going to do. Right now.

Oh, how well she knew him.

* * *

Shea, belting blindly away from the ballroom, smacked straight into Bryony, who looked exactly as she had on Skype, only eight inches taller.

'Great, just the person I was looking for! Wonderful to meet you at last, Shea!' Bryony thrust out her hand in greeting. 'Bryony Marshall, in case you haven't guessed already! Thanks so much for agreeing to stay on for the shoot, I'm so grateful, you've absolutely saved my life with that.'

And that was it. A moment later Bryony had dragged Shea into the whirl of her embrace, as if she'd known her forever, and was waltzing her towards the drawing room, chatting breathlessly as they went.

'You've done so amazingly here, I want to squeeze you, most of

151

all for taming Brando, that's simply the best news ever – it's such a pity Gloria won't see this in the flesh, but she's tied up presenting in Dublin, so we're going to shoot the footage and she'll add the voice-over later – the camera guys are arriving round lunchtime, but it's obviously more than ready – I can't believe what you've done, it all feels so different, like the house has sprung to life, and it's all down to you – I'm so excited I can't say.'

Shea's head reeled as they entered the haven of the newly finished drawing room, but the respite was short-lived.

'Wow, cool or what! Amazing work! Those funky sofas are so Brando – who'd have thought they'd look so at home next to the sash windows and the chandeliers – and the pale grey walls are a perfect complement – Brando must be over the moon.'

Bryony, the human dynamo. Impossible to resist, but despite her forceful approach, it was impossible not to be captivated by her gushing warmth and enthusiasm. Brando rarely mentioned Bryony without a desperate roll of his eyes and a grimace, and after five minutes in her company Shea understood why. The Skype chat they'd had before she came to Edgerton had given no clue to the enormity that was Bryony.

'About Brando...' Shea wondered if she needed to elaborate, given the cryptic nature of her call to Bryony earlier, but Bryony's reassuring hand landed heavily on her arm.

'Mrs McCaul gave me all the details when she rang to alert me.' She pushed artfully dishevelled blond hair behind her ear. 'Don't worry, Brando will get over it. It was always going to come as a shock, but he had to find out you're a widow at some stage, and he wouldn't be upset if he didn't adore you. He just needs time to get used to the idea, and he'll be fine.'

Brando adoring her? Shea's eyes sprung wide open at the very idea. *Jelly beans!* She dragged in an enormous breath, then shook her head, in perplexed desperation.

'No really, it's not like that...'

Was it?

What they shared last night, this morning even, had been scarily different. Her knees weakened.

Adoring? She *couldn't* go there.

She slammed a mental door on that one, hard and fast.

'You can't fool me. Look at what you've managed to get him to do here, all without protest, by all accounts. Plus you got him into bed, and I'm only referring to sleep here, not anything else. Any woman who managed to do that gets my whole-hearted respect – it can't have been easy. I know Brando, remember? He's stubborn as a mule, his own worst enemy, but you have the ability to persuade him to do what's good for him. I even heard him playing his guitar back there, and I'd never have believed that would happen, ever. It's one heck of an achievement so don't knock it!'

Shea, flinching at the mention of guitar playing, watched Bryony's face break into a wide, advert-perfect smile, which would have been totally intimidating on anyone less nice, and realised she wasn't going to get a word in edgeways.

'When I think how he cursed Gloria and her wife-on-a-postcard competition, but look what it's done for him. He's even spoken to our mother, and I'm darned sure he didn't do that on his own.'

'I knew he'd rung, but he didn't say they'd spoken.'

Bryony gave a long, despairing grunt. 'He wouldn't. This is Brando we're talking about, remember.'

If Shea hadn't felt so miserable she'd have had to smile at the way Bryony pulled a face, and rolled her eyes, just like Brando did whenever he talked about her. 'How are they getting on?'

'Well, it's baby steps on both sides. But they'll get there – thanks to you.'

Shea sensed that Bryony was about to pause for breath, and broke in, desperate to put her contribution into perspective, to set Bryony straight once and for all.

'What I've helped with at Edgerton, it's not that big a deal. It's only a few rooms. A sofa here, a few cushions there. Definitely nothing more. And a lorry load of flowers, of course. It's the flowers that make all the difference.'

Because that's what she was here for, and that's all she could cope with. It was all very well playing at being someone she wasn't, when she knew there weren't going to be any consequences. Being bad was great when you were someone else, and you knew it was going to end.

When you were in control.

Except last night she hadn't been. Not at all. And the thought of that still made her panic.

Bryony looked at her aghast, staring in a sudden, uncharacteristic silence. She chewed her thumb for a second, giving Shea a long, searching, quizzical glance, and when she finally spoke, her voice was low and disbelieving.

'Oh, my. You really *don't* get it do you?'

'What don't I get?' She kept her face straight, her expression impassive, even though she was dying inside. *If only...*

Bryony flashed her another radiant beam, grasped her elbow, steered her towards the door, and answered airily.

'It doesn't matter for now. Let's go and finish the flowers before the film guys arrive.'

* * *

'Well, that went brilliantly. Thanks so much for all your help, Shea, we got some great shots of you in the newly done rooms. The revisit programme covers the whole series, so it's going to be a whistlestop feature of Edgerton, about seven minutes of footage from before and after. As for Brando, when I get my hands on him, I will personally throttle him for running out on this!'

Shea's felt her stomach shrivel with guilt. 'It was fine. I'm sure they'll be able to make it look as if he was here, use film from before or something.'

She knew Brando's flight was down to their discussion in the ballroom, and although she wanted to leap in and defend him, taking responsibility would only make their entanglement seem more significant than it was.

'That's not the point!' Bryony's eyes flashed in annoyance. 'I know there's no love lost between him and Gloria, but I was counting on him to be here, and he knew that.'

Another wave of guilt shuddered through Shea, because Brando leaving had wiped out her problems with a stroke. This way there would be no goodbyes, no more worrying she was liking him too much. For a horrible moment when she woke this morning she'd thought she might be caring for him. *Falling for him even. Surely she'd* never *have let that happen?* But now he was gone – problem over – and by leaving, he'd only proven he was what she'd always thought. She hadn't hoped for any more, couldn't have coped if there had been more. And if a tiny part of her wanted more, she stamped on it hard. Because every time she thought about how she might have cared, she got a new squeeze of guilt about Greg, and that was a whole new ballgame which was best avoided.

Brando was *always* going to leave, and she'd *always* known that. It was the only reason she'd begun this in the first place. She couldn't have handled it any other way. At least now he'd gone she couldn't look at him to test how she felt. She wasn't sure any such test would have stood up to scrutiny. It was definitely better like this.

'So, it's all settled that you're staying until the end of the week to tie up the loose ends? Then we can get everyone who's been helping to come to a thank you party in the ballroom and we can all watch the programme together when it goes out next Sunday evening.'

Shea reeled. She'd been set on leaving, but she'd caved and agreed to stay on, in the face of Bryony's steam-roller style persuasion.

'Great! And after that I'm straight back to Manchester, to sort out a Mr and Mrs Cavanagh, who are downsizing to retirement accommodation.' Shea tried to beam enthusiastically at Bryony, tried to feel happy about going back to be with her friends and family, but as she thought of waking up back in her own bed instead of in Brando's at Edgerton, her smile failed miserably.

* * *

Champagne, canapés, big screens, invitations...

The to-do lists Bryony e-mailed to Shea on Monday were incessant and exhaustive, but Shea was grateful to have a stack of work to occupy her and threw herself headlong into it.

Music system, party tunes, balloons...

Tuesday, and still no word from Brando, though realistically she knew better than to expect it. A newsy e-mail or a chatty phone-call would hardly be his style. She knew that hoping for either was ridiculous after the rage he'd been in before he left, but she still couldn't stop her heart lurching at every ping of her inbox. She soldiered on with each new set of challenges, but somewhere down the line, her get up and go had got up and gone.

Celebration cupcake tower, napkins, bunting, new dress...

By Wednesday she'd become used to the constant ache in the pit of her stomach and although she refused to think about Brando, she had to admit through gritted teeth that despite the workload, which would usually have kept her ecstatic all week, without him, life at Edgerton had lost its zing.

She preferred too, to forget that deep in her wardrobe she had an old t-shirt of Brando's, scrunched up, stuffed under her stilettos. And she hated that each night, the only way she could sleep was if she took it out, and buried her face in it.

* * *

'Here Shea! Quick, grab some bubbly before we sit down.' Shea whipped around to see Bryony, head above the crowd, diamond earrings flashing in the light from the chandeliers, weaving her way

156

across the ballroom towards her in skin-tight purple suede and towering heels, holding two full to the brim champagne glasses aloft.

'Hey, thanks. It's crazy in here – quite a party!' Shea shouted above the din, and smiled gratefully as she took the glass from a flushed and excited Bryony.

'Are you okay? You're looking very pale. Pale, yet stunning, I have to say. Brando's going to love that slinky dress, peacock blue is *so* your colour. I hope I haven't been working you too hard?'

Shea's stomach did a double flip. If she was pale, she felt herself go several shades paler, as her insides sank to the floor. She tried for a throwaway tone, and just about pulled it off, apart from a telltale squeak of panic in her voice. 'I'm fine, really. I didn't know Brando was coming.'

Bryony's glanced impatiently at her watch, and tutted. 'He's cutting it a bit fine. We'd probably better encourage people to sit down, Edgerton's on first, we don't want to miss it!' Her eyes flashed fiercely as her gaze roved around the room. 'He's supposed to be sitting next to you! I'll murder the man single-handedly if he doesn't arrive!'

* * *

Twenty minutes later Shea was resting the palm of her hand on the velvet cushion of Brando's empty seat, eyes glued to the big screen, mesmerised. As she watched that familiar circling helicopter shot of Edgerton from the air, her throat began to constrict, and she knew it was a good thing Brando wasn't here. She swallowed hard, stuck a thumbnail between her teeth to chew on, and promised herself she wasn't going to cry.

A sudden shot of Brando filled the screen.

She whipped in her breath, dragged her arms around her ribs and felt one hot tear roll down her cheek and plop onto her knee. *Damn.*

Then just as she was brushing it off the hem of her dress, the jarring tones of Gloria Rutherford gushed through the air from the speakers like a shower of iced saccharine, and saved her. Shea shuddered back to normality, sniffed, scraped a finger under her lashes, praying that her mascara hadn't run, and began to concentrate on the screen again, only this time, thankfully, the images left her unmoved.

A sudden jab from an elbow landed in her ribs, and Bryony hissed at her in the gloom.

'Watch! This bit's new!'

Shea's eyes widened, as she saw a three second shot; Brando, with the deepest scowl ever, leaning over a table covered in postcards, picking one out. The camera zoomed in, and she let out an involuntary gasp as Brando held the card up to the camera, and the image of the telephone with a lobster receiver filled the screen. A sudden fizz of excitement infused her.

'My card! That was my card! So he did pick me!'

'Of course he picked you, silly!' Bryony's laughing voice was warm in her ear. 'Why else do you think you're here? You're here because he chose you! And I know your card said you had no matrimonial aspirations but I knew as soon as we spoke that you were just what Brando needed. That's why I was so insistent that you came.'

The rest of the film went by in a blur. Even though Shea was watching herself, it was as if she were watching someone else, and in no time Gloria's searing trill was ringing out in final conclusion.

'Brando's absence is clear indication that he has no interest in Edgerton, while Shea Summers has proved that she is capable of working miracles. Anyone else with a stately home in crisis, who would like to take advantage of her talents, we'd love to hear from you. She's a wonder woman, and we'd hate to see her qualities go unappreciated.'

And then it was all over, and a roar of applause rang out, and everyone got to their feet and cheered.

Chapter Eleven

The chauffeur driven car arrived at six o'clock the next morning, and an icy wind tore at Shea's hair, blowing it across her face as she hurried down the steps towards it.

Leave quickly and quietly in the dark, no looking back, no thinking how much it's going to hurt.

'You take care, and make sure you come back and see us.' Mrs McCaul gave Shea's shoulder a last pat as Bryony handed her bags to the driver.

Shea's lip trembled, and she chewed it hard, looking up, sticking her chin in the air as she swallowed away the saliva. She'd promised herself she was not going to cry, but now it came to it, leaving was going to be very hard. As she hugged herself to stem the ache which was gnawing in the pit of her stomach, through the blur of her tears she made out the flash of headlights racing between the trees on the drive and heard the roar of an approaching vehicle.

Her heart gave one huge lurch, then began to bang violently against her ribcage.

Only one person she knew made an engine scream like that, but surely it couldn't be? *Wanting it so much, yet terrified at the same time.*

There was a hideous squeal of brakes, and a shower of gravel, as the car screeched around the last bend, and skewed to a halt in front of them.

Shea forgot to breath.

And suddenly Brando was there, springing out of the car towards her, t-shirt flapping, dragging his fingers through his hair, turning her bones to jelly.

'Damned helicopters, damned fog! I should have been here twelve hours ago!'

Then he caught her in his arms, and she fell into the muscled wall of his embrace, as his hot mouth landed on hers and set her head spinning uncontrollably.

How she'd missed that.

She gave herself up to the glorious thrust of his tongue, let him draw her into his tumult of pleasure, until little by little her sensible self took over.

How she was going to miss that – that was the truth she needed to remember.

The sting of stubble dragged across her cheek as she pushed against his chest and broke away from his kiss. She drew in the dizzying smell of him, as she traced a finger across the familiar jut of his jaw, the amazing shadows of his cheekbones. Tried to pretend this was not for the last time.

'What the hell are you doing out here at this time of the morning anyway?' His rough tug on her hair jolted her back to earth, and as he gazed penetratingly into her eyes, she read a sudden desperation in his.

'I'm leaving Brando, I'm going home!' Her voice was quiet and firm, because suddenly she knew that going home was what was real. Her life wasn't about a stately pile and an impetuous man who catapulted in and out as he saw fit.

'You can't do that, not now! I want you here, I need you with me, dammit!' His voice was rising now and he took a step backwards, both hands tearing at his hair.

'You ran out Brando, and you were right to do that. We were always set to finish, and that way made it easier.' Her reply was low, yet decided. It could only be this way.

'The day I found out about Greg was awful, I behaved abominably, and I can only apologise. You're the one who's been through hell losing your husband, and I should have been talking to you about that, telling you how sorry I was, comforting you. But instead I ran. I ran out, because I was in shock. I'm not making excuses, I just want to explain. I thought I couldn't cope with being jealous of your dead husband. But, hell Shea, I was only jealous because I care about you. I've been fighting with myself. I always vowed I'd never put myself in a position where I'd feel jealousy ever again. It devours me, it makes me wild, you know that. But most of all I'm scared of it. I never planned to fall for you, dammit, I took every precaution not to. It was only when I found out about your husband that I realised exactly what I did feel for you. I was a total dumbass not to realise it before. My only excuse is I'm out of practice.' He sent her a boyish grin that made her heart squish. 'I left because I thought I couldn't bear to share you with a dead husband, because the jealousy was going to eat me up, but then I realised that not being with you was going to destroy me. So now I'm here, to tell you that I love you, and that I have to be with you, because I can't bear not to be with you.'

She planted a trembling hand on his arm in an effort to steady herself, as her chest began to constrict. He was here, he loved her. It should be perfect. Wasn't it what she'd secretly hoped in the darkest, deepest part of her? The teasing shimmers of anxiety that had been shivering through her as he spoke were building chaotically inside her. Blindly, she brushed a strand of hair away from her mouth and rubbed a hand across her forehead, because now he'd said it, it wasn't perfect. In fact nothing was right at all.

'But it's all decided. I have a job to go to, I'm going back to my life.' She was shuddering violently now, as panic gripped her.

What the hell was happening to her? During the last week when he hadn't been there, all she'd wanted to do was to bury herself in his arms. And every time before that it had been fine, because she'd always known he was a temporary measure, that there was no danger of him asking any more of her than she was giving, and that soon it would be over. The needling at her conscience, the low voice in her head, these told her it wasn't right for her to be having feelings so strong for someone who wasn't Greg... Telling herself that none of it mattered had kept her guilt neatly at bay. That was the whole essence of Brando, that was the kind of guy he was, and that was what had made him perfect, made him safe.

'I've thought about it, and I don't even mind marrying you, if that's what you want!'

His desperate words grated through the darkness, the absurdity of his statement stemming her panic momentarily.

'Nice proposal, great style Brando, but no thanks. You already know I don't want that!' He was here, laying it on the line, so how mean was she to be throwing it back in his face? But now it came to it, she couldn't cope.

His snort suggested some people couldn't be pleased, but his face crumpled into an agonised expression, which swiftly morphed to anger. 'You can't turn your back on what we've got! I won't let you.'

She watched him, assessing his pent up energy, the annoyance that threatened to explode at any moment, as he slammed his toe into the gravel. A Brando who didn't care, she could manage. A Brando who did care was beyond her. There was no way she could handle that. She hadn't signed up for love. Love was exactly what she *couldn't* do, and the thought of it made her want to run for the hills.

All she hoped for was that he didn't start looking lost and vulnerable. If he did that she wouldn't stand a chance. She needed to wrap this up fast and get out of here, say whatever was needed to achieve that.

'You've got it all wrong.' She half closed her eyes, braced herself to lie. 'Let's face it – we had a fifteen minute fling that got out of hand, it was pretty much burned out anyway when you left.'

The flying punch he threw into the air with one tightly wound fist whipped his body around.

'That's rubbish and you know it! The last night was...'

Her heart jumped two beats as he said that. She couldn't let him go there. Only her lightning interjection cut him off.

'That night was not important.'

Hold it together. She owed it to them both, she had to go now. Because the moment he told her he loved her it changed everything. And now, all the guilt about Greg was rushing down on her again, tumbling like a waterfall in flood.

'I'm leaving, Brando, I have to go, and I'm sorry, but nothing you say will change my mind!' She took a step towards the waiting car and opened the door decisively, knowing she couldn't waver.

'Have it your own way, Miss Shea-do-as-I-say!' He was yelling now, taunting, leaning forwards, his face contorted in anger. 'Walk away if you must, but I guarantee you'll be back. We've both invested too much here for you to leave. You should be with me; we belong together. Just don't count on me giving up!'

The wind buffeted the words away, as she fumbled her way blindly into the back seat of the car. There was no way could she acknowledge any of what he was saying. He'd jumped too far, and forced her to fast forward to a place she couldn't be. Ever. Behind her she heard a thump as he hurled the last suitcase into the boot.

Then the boot lid slammed with an ear-hammering crash, the car slid into the darkness, and just as she'd promised herself, she didn't look back.

And that was that.

* * *

Shea picked her way across the living room with her pizza, sighing in despair at the tangle of hair-straightener cables and discarded pizza boxes. She sent her housemate Tasha the biggest smile she could muster under the circumstances, and wondered where Guy and Ellie were.

Tasha gave a return grin as she looked up from tweezing her eyebrows. 'So Sunday night, pampering night, just like old times. Throw me that nail varnish and tell me what's new!'

Shea picked up the blue nail varnish she'd been using earlier, tossed it to Tasha, then flopped into a chair, tucked her legs underneath her and began to rearrange the towel that swathed her wet hair.

'Oh, same old, same old. Spending this week and next sorting out a downsize, but the good news is I've got a twelve week block booking with no details as yet, but that'll take me into March.' She forced herself to take a bite of a slice of pizza, realising her best efforts to sound enthusiastic had crashed. 'It's very quiet here, where is everybody?'

'Things have changed since that Sunday we all sat here filling in those postcards. Talk about everyone getting a life! Ellie's taken up pole dancing, Guy's gone for a drink with this week's Mr Right.'

Shea watched Tasha's wistful sigh in silence, knowing Tasha was also desperate for a Mr Right, knowing there were some Mr Rights who were best avoided because they could wring out your heart without even trying. Send you to places as awful as the one where she was now – she'd had the most awful week, trying to pick up the pieces. There was a searing pain where her chest used to be, she'd barely slept or eaten and as her clients, poor Mr and Mrs Cavanagh, were aware, she was failing to keep her mind on the job at work. The jangle of the doorbell pulled her back to earth.

'Damn, who can that be? I'll go, seeing as you're in your dressing gown.' Tasha peered out of the bay window as she passed, and Shea saw her eyes widen. 'Wow! Some hunk who looks like he got lost on the way to a Vogue shoot.'

Shea leaned across to get a better view, puzzled as she took in the unexpected, yet unmistakable profile.

'Brando?' She clasped a fist to her mouth, as her insides imploded. 'Walnut whips! What's he doing here?'

Apart from her wide open eyes, the fact she kept opening and closing her mouth like a goldfish and had a face the colour of chalk, Brando noted as he shuffled into the room, Shea was making a good job of taking his unscheduled visit in her stride.

'Excuse the chaos, mind you don't get caught up in the hair-straighteners, sit down if you can find somewhere. How come you're in Manchester?'

Brando gave a casual shrug. 'Oh, you know, just passing.'

Not.

He stared around at the chaos of strewn towels and cosmetics, as Shea's friend hurried out of the room, clutching her hair-straighteners, and over the thump of his racing pulse he heard the door click closed.

'Nice place!' He flung an ice-breaking grin in Shea's direction, raised an eyebrow towards the mess, dropped his jacket on the sofa, and squatted down, resting his forearms on his thighs. 'I take it the housemates got out of hand when Miss Tidy-freak wasn't here to keep them in line?'

Despite being aware of the judder of his own breathing, he failed to steady it.

She sniffed, and rolled her eyes. 'It's always like this on Sundays after a weekend of debauchery. You know how it is.'

'I guess.' He shrugged again, twisting his face into a grimace. The whole point was he didn't know, he had no idea what her life was like when she wasn't at Edgerton. 'So how have you been?'

'Good, thanks.'

That reply was too pat. Was it too much to hope the fact she was looking pale and drawn was down to her missing him, or was it just that she hadn't put on her make-up since she got out of the shower?

'You smell nice.' That slipped out before he could help himself and he swallowed back how wonderful it was to see her again.

All he wanted to do was rush over, drag her into his arms, and never let her go, but her fierce expression warned him to keep his distance. Or else.

She studied him with guarded eyes, as she unwound the towel from her head, and shook out the long damp wavy strands of her hair. 'How did you know where to find me?'

'Your mother told me you'd be...'

'My mother?' She jumped down his throat, her brow wrinkled in a frown of disbelief.

Mistake number one to let that out. 'Yep, I've been ringing her every day to see how you are.'

'Brando!'

He heard the slightest tinge of humour in her scolding. Maybe she wasn't quite as glacial as she was pretending.

'I'm not backing off on this one.' He gritted his teeth, recognising for a fleeting second the same dogged determination he brought to his business deals. 'So now we're here, and you've had a week to think about it, and it isn't six o'clock on a windy morning, I want you to look me in the eye and tell me, honestly, that you don't want to be with me.'

'It's not like that, you don't understand.'

He turned on her, with a jubilant slap of his thigh. 'There you go, I knew you couldn't say it! And that's because you *do* want to be with me!'

She stared back at him impassively through narrowed wary eyes, chewing her bottom lip, but said nothing.

'So where's the problem?'

This time she simply sniffed, shuffled sulkily, and didn't meet his eye.

'Come on, we all have our skeletons, things we have to overcome. We can't always do it on our own. Jeez, if anyone knows that it's me.'

He rubbed his thumbnail over the twitching muscle in his cheek. She wasn't going to crack easily. Where the hell had bolshy, bossy,

166

do-as-I-say-Shea disappeared to?

'The thing is, I'm back, my life here is sorted, I've just committed to a three month work booking and I'm settled.'

'Anything interesting?'

'I don't know the details as yet, only that the offer was too good to turn down.'

'Oh, right.' He nodded obliquely. 'You know Shea, you can come back and live your life, pretend everything is okay, but sooner or later your demons will be back to haunt you, I guarantee it. Hell, if anyone knows that to their cost, it's me.'

'You would say that, wouldn't you.'

'You were the one who made me talk about mine, remember? You were the one who told me that facing my demons was the only way to conquer them. Where would I be now if I'd stonewalled like you're doing?'

Her only reply was a disgruntled snort as she propped her chin on her hand. Watching her strawberry pout quivering, he longed to crash his mouth over it, make everything okay again, but right now that would be folly. God, he hoped he could explain, talk her round, make this work, because who knew what he was going to do if he couldn't?

'The point is you helped me. You helped me get back in touch with my mother, helped me come to terms with all the stuff about the accident, the reason I hated Edgerton. You made me feel secure, happy enough to sleep again. But you helped me because I let you, and it's only fair that you let me help you too. I know the way I reacted when I found out about Greg was unforgivable. I was uncompassionate and selfish, and I can't blame you if you hold that against me. You have been through so much pain and grief and suffering, but hell, you deserve another chance to be happy, and if I have it in my power to help you do that, I will. But you have to let me.'

He watched her chomping on her thumbnail, like a stubborn child in a strop, forcing himself to ignore how her robe had slipped,

167

to give him an uninterrupted take on the delicious curve of her right breast. *He'd missed her so much; this had to work.* A slight shift in her position cut off his sight line.

Damn.

'If it hadn't been for you, I'd never have picked up a guitar again, and I'd still be sleeping in the office chair, dammit. And I wouldn't be desperate to spend my life with a woman. So you, and your advice about facing demons, have got a hell of a lot to answer for.'

There was still no shift in her tight lipped pout. Right now he didn't know what he wanted to do most – shake her or kiss her.

'With your help, I overcame all that stuff. At the time, I knew you understood me better than anyone else in the world, but it's only now I know the reason you understood so well. All the pain you'd been through yourself let you reach out to help me, touch me in a way no-one else could. But that last demon of all was the killer – the rest were nothing compared to that. Me with my jealous streak, finding out that you loved a man who was dead, that damned nearly destroyed me. That last one was the monster of all demons – so huge it made me ignore all your needs, and become totally obsessed with my own. If you had any idea of the number of buildings I had to jump off to get to grips with that one...'

He felt the catch in his throat, watched her eyes narrow as she reacted to the sudden faltering of his voice, but he battled on, fighting to get the words out because these were the words he had been aching to tell her.

'You loving him explained why you were always so anxious for the end to come for us. At first the jealousy ate me up, but then I remembered how you told me jealousy was the most destructive emotion. Then I began to face it and to beat it. I had every motivation to because if I didn't, there was no chance of being with you at all, and I couldn't bear the idea of that.'

* * *

In silence she lowered her eyes, clasped her arms around her ribs as she heard the swagger leech out of Brando, sensed the arrogance drop away, leaving only low imploring tones as he went on.

'And so I know now that you will always love him, and I'm okay with that, because I've decided that even if you only have a little bit of love left over to give as you move on to the future, however small that is, I have to be the one you give that love to. I love you, Shea, I have to be with you....'

She took a long, juddering breath. She'd missed Brando so much since they'd been apart. The day Brando left, the colour left her world and she'd felt physically ill with her need for him. And Brando saying he loved her now was the scariest thing in the world. But at the same time, deep, deep down, it was what she'd ached to hear but never allowed herself to hope for. She knew, after what she'd done, that she didn't deserve love ever again. She dared herself to raise her eyes.

Slowly. Up. Past the muscled denim thighs, the strong clasp of his fingers, over the faded folds of his shirt, the rugged column of his throat. *Achingly slowly.* Over the jagged thrust of his jaw, the sculpted shadows of his cheekbones. And then their eyes met, and her stomach did a triple flip – because the eyes that looked back at her weren't the assured flinty eyes of a powerful man, but the cloud-grey eyes of an imploring, vulnerable boy.

That was all it took.

'I feel sick!' Simultaneously Shea tried to bury her moan, and quash the butterfly wings beating wildly in her chest, knowing that every last shred of resistance had seeped from her. She'd tried to fight it for so long, tried so hard to deny this heart-wringing, earth shaking feeling, that possessed every fibre of her being, even to herself.

'Might that be because you love me, just a little bit?' He studied her quizzically, the deep pools of his eyes turning her bones to syrup, as he rubbed a thumb pensively over his jaw, then extended an expectant hand towards her.

She shrank, quivering, back into her chair. There was so much she needed to explain.

'I can't do love, Brando. That's what you don't understand. I can't love you, I can't love anyone, because I'm simply not capable of it.' Whatever the strength of the tidal wave of emotion gripping her body, she couldn't trust herself to love Brando as he deserved.

'Come here and tell me about it. I can't concentrate when you're so far away.' His face slid into a gentle smile that made her insides flip again, and he sprung forwards. She suppressed a shiver as his strong, firm fingers entwined with hers, tugging her insistently towards the sofa where he'd been sitting.

'Please? It'll be easier when you're next to me.'

Those soft smudged charcoal eyes could make her do anything; her bodyweight was her only resistance now. One tug from Brando, they both hit the sofa, and her dizzy head crashed against the glorious rock of his shoulder.

'Now, try and tell me why you can't love me.'

It was hard when the heat of his body was infusing deep into her core, and the battering of his heartbeat and the dark musky scent of him were derailing her concentration completely.

Try not to think how perfect it feels to be in his arms. Not yet. How being back in his arms feels so much like coming home, home to where you want to be forever. Not when you can't give what it takes to be in that place.

She inhaled deeply. Once she'd come clean, Brando would understand. 'When I tried to love Greg, I failed him completely.'

'In whose eyes?'

The vigour of his challenge shocked her, and fired a note of protest into her weary voice.

'It wasn't like you think, it wasn't like anybody thought. Greg and I grew up together. Our families were close, then the summer I was eighteen, he came back from uni and we started hanging out together. It was later that year he started getting symptoms. It took a while, but eventually he was diagnosed with a brain tumour. When we found out he wasn't going to get better, we got married. But everything went so fast – the fact they're fit and strong makes the illness take hold faster. But the person who died wasn't the Greg I knew. As the illness bit, he became bitter and angry and difficult, and in the end he came to hate me, and I couldn't handle it. When it came to the test, my love for him wasn't anywhere near big enough or good enough.'

'I doubt anyone would have coped as well with a situation like that!' His sympathetic hand found her bare leg, tucked up underneath her now and he grasped her ankle, scraped a nail across her skin, continuing urgently. 'It doesn't mean you can't love. Under different circumstances, better ones, I already know you have more than enough love to give. Hell, you've already showered me with love enough to help me through my problems! You just didn't see it as love at the time.'

She dismissed his reassurance with a half shake of her head.

'You haven't heard the bad bit yet – the worst thing is that when he died, I was glad. I wasn't sorry; all I felt was relief. And worse still was that everyone thought I should be devastated, when actually I was happy to be free, because it had all been so terrible. How awful is that? What sort of person does that make me?'

'It makes you a real, human person, Shea, but not a bad one. You were coping with a traumatic loss. Grief drives us to extremes, we react unpredictably, feel crazy things. And it's okay, it's just a normal part of the hell of it all.' Brando's soft growl, gently justifying what she'd done.

'I've never thought of it like that.'

'Love is about helping each other through situations, and understanding, and being able to forgive when it doesn't go right. You understood Greg couldn't help being as he was. He would have forgiven you too, if he could have. You've been beating yourself up about it for too long. It's time to give yourself a break.' Brando rubbed away her pain like no-one else ever had.

'Maybe...'

Then his arms were around her, closing around her ribcage, holding her tightly as her body heaved and shuddered, and the tears that had been so long in coming soaked deep into his t-shirt. When she finally found her voice again it was small and scratchy.

'I haven't told anyone before, I was too ashamed. And I couldn't even cry either.' She sniffed, dragging her sleeve across the blotchy redness of her cheek. 'All I could do was work, but then I couldn't stop.'

'I knew there had to be a reason, Miss Work-all-day-Shea. I had your number, you know.'

His gruff voice resonated beneath her face, still clamped to his chest.

'You've no idea what a relief it was when I got away, and came to Edgerton where no-one knew. Because all these years people have tiptoed around me, trying not to upset me, trying to be considerate, whilst I was being a total fraud. Because the day Greg died, I wasn't sad, or devastated, I was relieved. Who would ever want to be with a person like that?'

'I can think of one person who wouldn't mind at all.'

His reply came, low and laid-back, as he combed his fingers through the damp strands of her hair, nudging her head so he could see her. How like this wonderful, understanding man to make her feel as if her heart was about to burst.

'But then there's the way I feel so guilty.' Somehow just saying the word out loud eased the crippling tension which had been twisting her gut into knots for days. 'So long as what we had was temporary it was easy, because none of it mattered. But the morning I was leaving Edgerton, when you told me that you cared, that flipped everything on its head. Somehow, you talking about love made everything I'd been denying seem real. And not only those feelings existing, but how strong they were, made me feel so guilty – guilty for feeling so strongly about you, when I should have been feeling that about Greg. All the guilt I'd been holding back and ignoring this whole time came crashing down on me.'

Brando, eyes dark with thought, wrinkled his brow. 'I think it's natural for you to feel guilty. But what you feel now, won't ever take away from what you and Greg had. That will always be special, part of your life, part of you, and I'll always respect that. I'm just happy to have whatever you have to give to me. I already know it's enough, but I also know I can't live without it.'

'Thank you for saying that Brando. In my heart of hearts, I know Greg would want me to be happy and to start living again. And I know that I'm ready. I think that's what I proved when I came to Edgerton.'

'I think so too.' He trailed a finger across her cheek.

'I'm very pleased I came.' She was filled with the strangest sensation, as her worries and fears began to melt away to nothing.

'So am I.' As he rubbed his cheekbone against hers, the tingling abrasion sent darts of desire skittering through her.

She was aware of a warm syrupy heat pooling in the base of her stomach. It had to be because she was sitting, curled up safe, next to the man she was going to be spending her life with. He'd somehow given her something she thought she'd never have again – the chance to love. And he'd shown her, not only that he wanted to love her, but that she was completely capable of loving him. She swallowed one huge gulp, dragged in a giant breath, and braced herself to say the words, because if anyone deserved to know, it was Brando.

'I love you, Brando.'

Brando turned her face to his, rubbed a broad thumb across her cheek to catch her tears. 'You've no idea how happy it makes me to hear that.'

'I'm sorry it took me so long to say it. You've made me happy for the first time in years, happier than I've been in fact, ever.' Her voice wavered against his cheek. 'Now I know I can love you, and it's alright to love you, I never ever want to leave you, and I'll do my best to love you forever.'

He pulled her mouth to meet his kiss.

Sweet, rough, strong. Very hot, and long. When he finally broke away, his voice was deliciously ragged against her ear.

'I love you Shea, I love who you are, and what you do. Your love is more than good enough for me – you've already proved that. I already know you're who I need, who I want to spend my life with. And I bet there's never been a Lady of the Manor at Edgerton with electric blue toe nails before!' He tweaked one toe, tapped his temple teasingly against hers. 'Perhaps you could be the first?'

She felt her face stretch into a smile.

' Thank you Brando, that would be amazing and wonderful. So long as you're sure you understand who you're taking on, there's nothing I'd like more.' She let out a sudden groan as her mind whirled. 'But I've just committed to a three-month contract.'

'Okay, I'm going to have to come clean on that one.' He pursed his lips, grimaced as he hesitated. 'My P.A. booked you for that. I couldn't bear to think of you being tied up elsewhere, and not being with me, and if all this had backfired, at least I'd have known you were working back at Edgerton, with plenty of excuses to drop in on you. I'm very thorough, and very determined. I had every aspect covered.' He shot her a smile. 'Not that I'm wanting you to work, but knowing how you hate having nothing to do, I was hoping you might like to come and sort out the building in London. It's a converted warehouse with a penthouse flat, a few thousand square feet of bachelor chaos with my offices below, which hasn't had the benefit of Mrs McCaul's attention. There should be enough there to keep you going for years! And we can spend time at Edgerton too, obviously. We have such a great time when we're there together, I'd love for us to live there and have some kids. Now see what you've done to the guy who wouldn't leave London, and thought he could never change.'

'Awwww, Brando. I do love you, very much.' She added a hasty afterthought. 'And not just because you've offered me endless amounts of organising to do. I'm not sure that you or Edgerton are ready for children though.'

'I think we're about to prove you wrong.' He shot her a smile that flipped her tummy. Again. 'One more thing. The reason I came.' He fumbled in the pocket of his jacket, pulled out a postcard, and flipped it towards her. 'Apparently Bryony's Country House Crisis programme has been inundated with enquiries about you taking your talents to other stately homes. I wanted to make sure I got in first, before you had chance to consider the opposition!'

As she looked at the picture on the card her crazily wide smile, broadened further.

'Awww, Brando! It's Dali's Mae West lips sofa! He made that sofa for the same patron he made the lobster telephones for. This card matches the one I sent in!'

He nodded at her knowingly, and winked.

'That's why I chose it, duh, although I never actually read what you wrote on your card at the time. Bryony tells me you claimed on the card to have no matrimonial aspirations, so I'm sorry I gave you such a hard time at first for you being a husband hunter. Turn it over, and read the message.'

'Brando Marshall would like to be considered' A sudden whoosh took her voice away as she read on. For a moment her nose stung horribly, and she bit her lip. *Keep calm and carry on.* Gulping down the spiky taste of tears she kept going. '...would like to be considered for the position as Shea Summer's husband...' She sent him a wavering smile, as she rubbed a tear from the corner of her eye '...because he's the only man for the job!'

'The thing is I'd really like you to marry me, if you'd like to, that is?' He shot her a wicked grin.

'Awwwwww Brando!' She leaned across and grabbed a handful of tissues from the coffee table, and blew her nose loudly. 'I can't believe you just asked me to marry you – my hair is all wet, I'm not wearing any knickers, and I'm crying.'

'No knickers, I can definitely work with, once you've answered that is!' His lips twitched in appreciation, as he raised one questioning, slightly impatient eyebrow. 'So what do you say....

Shea, will you marry me?'

'I'd love to, Brando!' She flashed him a mischievous glance. 'So long as you're ready to do as you're told. You do know how bossy I am when I'm not snivelling, that is.'

'I damn well do! And right now, after two weeks without you, I'll pretty much promise to do anything you say, so long as you let me take you to bed right now!'

In one leap, Brando was up, and she felt the room spin as he grasped her in his arms, threw her into the air, and whirled her around.

She let out one shriek of surprise, which happily, he ignored, and then she gave in to the delicious thrill, and pure exuberance of his raw embrace.

'I've loved you since the moment I saw you and hauled you into the house the day you arrived by helicopter, and I'm going to carry on loving you. But right now I need to ravish you!' He swept her across the room, and with one easy swing of his knee he opened the door.

'Brando! That day, I knew the instant you picked me up that you were completely special, just from the way you made my stomach spin, and I guess that's when I fell in love with you too. You turned my whole life upside down, and you've been shaking me every day since. You could say it was love at first lift.' She grinned right on up at him, as his erection bumped on her bottom.

'Sounds right to me.' He looked down at her adoringly through sooty lashes, and made her heart squish again. 'Now point me in the direction of your bedroom, and I'll show you how much I love you!'